THE
SCAVENGER

J. L. Willow   6/2/18

J L Willow

NEBULA
PRESS

The Scavenger

Nebula Press. For any questions about usage, please contact us at nebulapressbooks@yahoo.com or visit our website: www.nebulapressbooks.com.

Visit the author's website at www.jlwillow.com or contact her at jlwillowbooks@gmail.com.

First Edition.

ISBN 10: 0-9992526-0-7
ISBN 13: 978-0-9992526-0-4

This is a work of fiction. All of the characters, organizations, and events portrayed in this novel are either products of the author's imagination or are used fictitiously. Any correlations to real life are purely coincidental.

Cover design by Damonza.com

Author Photograph © Danuta Amato

10   9   8   7   6   5   4   3   2   1

To Mama and Padre,
Thank you for believing in Squigmire.

The struggle of life is one of our greatest blessings. It makes us patient, sensitive, and God-like. It teaches us that although the world is full of suffering, it is also full of overcoming it.

– Helen Keller

The Scavenger

To: mpeeler@uvhs.org
From: ntawallis@nypd.org
Subject: Update on Network Situation

Principal Peeler,

Good afternoon. My name is Nathan Tawallis. I'm a detective in the Narcotics Division of the New York City Police Department assigned to your district. We appreciate your reaching out to us regarding the situation in your school system. We are still investigating the two recent overdoses by students and will disseminate information as it becomes available. With regard to your concerns, let me present the facts to you as they currently stand.

Toxicology reports have revealed that the drug involved in the two overdoses was laced marijuana. Although these two incidents may seem like a coincidence, we have reason to believe otherwise. As more states legalize marijuana, we've seen an increasing number of young people participating in its usage. Dealers now see this an opportunity to introduce their clients to more addictive drugs by lacing marijuana with other substances. Although this is new to the Unison Valley school district, it is not new to the drug world. A few years ago, a strain emerged in South Africa titled "Swazi Gold." This cannabis has dangerously high THC levels and it was discovered that once mixed with cocaine, it became extremely addictive. It is a possibility that this mix, or something similar to this, has been introduced to your school. To students who have only used pure or unlaced marijuana, their bodies are unprepared for the powerful additives that come with the mix. It is common for dealers to withhold from their users that the product they're being provided is laced, a trick used to give them something more addictive without their knowledge. This would explain the two cannabis-related overdoses in such a short period of time.

Our department has several leads that are being investigated. Your students' safety is our highest priority. If any peculiar activity occurs regarding this issue or you have any additional concerns, don't hesitate to contact me.

We will keep you informed on this issue as much as possible, sending updates and correspondences regularly.

Nathan Tawallis, NYPD

1 CATHERINE

"You're doing it again."

Throwing Eve a look, I kicked one of the numerous pebbles littering the sidewalk. It skidded forward and ricocheted off the wall of a small pub before spinning to a stop. "Doing what?"

"You're zoning out. Did you even hear what I said?"

"Yeah." There were a few seconds in which I tried — and failed — to recall Eve's last words. "Well, maybe. But I'm listening now."

A fresh gust of wind pushed a lock of curly red hair askew from the bun perched at the top of her head. Eve scrunched the skin around her pale blue eyes in annoyance before pushing it back in its proper place. "I asked you if you wanted to come to the mall with me. You know? For those spring sales?"

Keeping my eyes on the sidewalk, I answered, "I think I'll pass. I'm kinda running low on funds right now."

"That's what window-shopping is for." When I neglected to reply, my friend grabbed me by my backpack and pulled me to a stop. "Hey, what's up with you? I just brought up the prospect of mall-time and you're treating it like it's no big whoop."

"There's nothing up with me." I yanked myself forward to break Eve's grip, then continued walking. My friend let out a huff before striding to walk beside me again. "I just don't feel like going right now. That's all."

It was a quiet morning, an uncommon occurrence considering our location in upper New York. The city's movements rarely slowed enough for its residents to enjoy a few quiet minutes, let alone a morning stroll to the nearby high school. Currently, though, I was having trouble enjoying it thanks to Eve's constant probing.

"Catherine." My friend's voice was strained. "I don't know what's been up with you recently. I'm getting worried about you." She cared so much about everything. If only she would stop caring long enough to try to understand.

"Worried about what?" I said evenly. "I'm doing fine. Great, even."

"I mean, with the divorce and everything..." My expression caused the sentence to die on her lips. She swallowed before saying, "I'm sorry, I shouldn't have brought that up. But you really should talk to someone about everything that's been going on."

"I'm not a child, Eve. I can take care of myself."

"I'm not saying that you can't, it's just…" Eve shook her head as if to clear it, giving me a sheepish grin. "Sorry. You know me, the mom-friend. Always overstepping my boundaries. I just want to make sure you're doing okay."

After a moment, I smiled my forgiveness. Eve meant well, even if she didn't know what she was talking about some of the time. "You don't have to worry about me."

"You know what would make me worry less?" I really didn't care to know, but Eve continued nonetheless. "If you got yourself involved in something."

"Like what?"

"I don't know. Something. Anything. A club, a sport, a relationship—"

"A *relationship?*"

"Sure! You haven't dated anyone in forever."

"Seventh grade," I interjected. "I had a boyfriend in seventh grade. That was only two years ago."

"No one counts their *middle school boyfriends*." Unwilling to engage in another round of tug-of-war, Eve pushed in front of me and placed two hands on my shoulders. I teetered slightly while attempting to balance the weight of my textbooks. "Catherine, listen to me. You need to loosen up, try something new. It'll help take your mind off everything. You're only in high school once," she threw her arms up, "so live a little!"

"I've already *lived* through too many of these conservations." I stepped around her, using my height advantage to put some distance between us. "And quit cutting in front of me. We're going to be late."

Eve heaved a sigh of annoyance, then lightly jogged to catch up. "Why are you dead-set on leading the most boring, mundane life possible?"

Looking away from her accusing eyes, I nudged another rock with my foot without breaking stride. "The way you're putting it sounds like I'm a lazy bore that'll be living in my mom's basement for ten years."

My friend shrugged. "No comment."

"Shut up! I'm not like that."

Seeing she wasn't getting anywhere with her playful jabs, Eve offered, "Okay, maybe you're partially not. But you have to admit your routine is desperately in need of something new."

Surrendering to her persistence, I stopped walking and placed my hands on my hips. "Okay, fine. Since you're so sure you know everything, what should I do?"

Eve smiled, putting up a finger as she prepared to speak.

I watched the gears turn behind her eyes. After a moment, she said, "I'll get back to you on that."

"Really?" A car passed us on the road, swallowing my exclamation in the grumble of its engine. When the noise dissipated, I huffed, "Eve, you can't tell me I need to change and then have no idea on what to change."

"I said I'd get back to you! I'll come up with something." She cocked her head at me with a smirk. "Remind me: how long have we been friends?"

She was going to play that card again. "Eight years," I replied in monotone.

"And how many times has my intuition come in handy?"

"A lot."

"Uh huh. Like that one time in school you wanted to try that hummus platter and I told you not to and saved your life?"

"You said I shouldn't eat it because it looked gross, not because it was life-threatening. We didn't find out I was allergic to chickpeas until way later."

"Ah!" Eve pointed at me triumphantly. "*Intuition!*"

"Whatever. Well, when your 'gifted intuition' decides to strike again, let me know."

Eve punched my shoulder lightly. "You know I will. Maybe something big will come and jazz up your life a little, you know?"

"Uh huh, sure," I muttered. What did she honestly think was going to happen? We weren't living in some sort of fantasy where the perfect guy appeared out of nowhere. I'd learned the hard way that life rarely provided happy endings.

2 FRANK

A bell gave a shrill cry and I jolted awake. Vague wisps of dreams fled my mind as I blinked away the sunlight. Checking the clock blinking on the dashboard, I realized I must have fallen asleep. I wasn't surprised; I'd been pulling some pretty late nights recently. My gaze stopped on the man staring back at me in the rearview mirror.

Contrary to the fact that I barely had three decades under my belt, the bags hanging under my eyes added at least another five years to my face. Nickie was always telling me I needed more sleep. Maybe it was time to listen to her nagging. A yawn confirmed her hypothesis. Deciding I couldn't do anything more about it at the moment, I settled back and watched the students pour out of the school. Their loud chatter was filtered to a low murmur through the walls of the car.

Every time I visited the high school, I glimpsed the same scene. Small giggling cliques of girls tossed their too-blonde hair and made a bee-line for a nearby coffee shop. Jocks wearing matching blue and yellow varsity jackets hauled their gym bags while lightly rough-housing their teammates. Others walked side by side, eyes thick with liner and unnaturally dyed hair cropped short. I found it fascinating how they all stayed in their little groups. They all thought they were so *unique*, when really there were hundreds just like them in countless other high schools. I knew the one I was keeping an eye out for wouldn't be found among them. He didn't fit into any of those categories. He was a bit more subtle.

The boy stood apart from the crowd. Although he walked alone, his posture held the loose sureness of confidence. I saw his expression shift when he spotted my black vehicle. He immediately changed direction and began striding toward me. I chuckled as he pulled in vain at the locked passenger-side door. It was only after he started staring daggers at me that I slowly moved to unlock it.

"What are you doing here?" McGee hissed, flinging his bag into the backseat. "You know I don't like it when you show up like this."

"When have I ever taken orders from you?" I feigned a charming smile. "How was school today, son?"

"I'm not your son."

I shrugged. "I'd like to think we're like family now, after all these years." Receiving no response, I continued, "Anyway, you can probably guess that I came here for a reason."

McGee narrowed his eyes at me. "Is it about that *Times* article?"

"So you did see that." He was learning, keeping his eyes peeled. A good sign of his development. "Nice thought, but no. Don't worry about that just yet. I'm here about something more important. Your newest subject, to be exact."

"Oh." The kid glanced around as if someone could hear us through the doors of the car. "What about him?"

"How is it progressing?'

"Progressing?" McGee answered. "It's done. He's completely hooked. I wouldn't be surprised if he's one of our top buyers within the next few weeks."

I gave him a look. "So it would be safe to say that you're excelling in this new position."

"Hell yeah I am. These last three assignments have been a piece of cake."

"And that," I interrupted, "is the exact reason I'm here. You're getting cocky."

McGee snorted. "A little confidence never hurt anyone. You seem to have a surplus of it yourself."

The comeback itself was case in point. I was giving the kid too much slack. He needed to be put in place. His arrogance had the possibility of backfiring against me, and then I would find myself in deep shit with the police. I stared pointedly at the students loitering around the schoolyard. "I need to knock you down a few pegs, kid. I'm choosing your next subject. Here and now."

"Now?" The kid's eyebrows raised in surprise. "I don't think these are quite the type of people we're—"

"You said it yourself," I interjected. "These last few have been far too easy for you. Besides, I've been thinking about trying to expand our operation. We can start now." I skimmed the crowd, then gestured to a pair of students walking side by side. "That one."

McGee turned to look. "Which one?"

"Dark hair."

"What?" he protested. "I think we only have a class or two together."

"Not my problem." An idea popped into my head. "Even better, let's raise the stakes. You up for a bet?"

That caught his attention. "A bet?"

"Yeah." I thought for a moment. "Five-spot says you can't get that one into the system in less than a month."

McGee straightened. "$500?"

"No more, no less."

"On top of my regular commission?"

"Yeah, what the hell? I'm feeling generous."

Blowing out a whistle, the kid sat back slowly. Then he stuck out his hand. "It's a deal."

We shook. "I knew you wouldn't let me down." As I shifted the car into drive, I gave him a sharp smile. "You know what else I was thinking about? You need a code name."

"A what?"

"A code name. Something that fits you. You know — I'm a Dealer, Victor's a Wholesaler, etcetera. You're just 'the back-stabbing sneak that befriends the target I tell you to and gets 'em hooked on my product.' Doesn't quite flow off the tongue." I spread my hands wide, mimicking a name in lights. "How about *Scavenger?* That sounds good to me. Plus, it's a step up from your glorified delivery-boy title."

McGee took his eyes off the students to throw me a look. "And what exactly am I 'scavenging'?"

"Whoever I damn well please. It's a loose translation."

"Call me whatever you want, just get your money ready," muttered McGee, head turned toward the school once more.

Giving a chuckle, I stuck the key into the ignition and turned it. The engine purred as we pulled onto a side-street, leaving the students to disappear in the rearview mirror. "Alright, Scavenger. Let's get you home."

3 NATHAN

"He published it in the *Times*?"

"What did you expect him to do? You wanted people informed, so this is how you get it done."

I bit my lip, attempting to control the rage that threatened to boil over. "There was a reason I transferred the information by private email and not public transcript. I was *expecting* a school newsletter, or an informational meeting. This was supposed to be kept quiet, not broadcasted throughout the city!"

"Honestly, I don't know why you're making such a big deal about this. He was bound to inform the community when the illegal marijuana industry is such a big issue. You can't expect him to keep them completely in the dark about this." I was painfully aware that Therese's points were legitimate. It didn't ease my agitation as I paced back and forth in front of her desk.

Therese watched, leaning back to teeter on the back legs of her chair before placing her hands delicately behind her head. She had dainty features, hardly showing her age of nearly thirty-five. Her face held only the faintest of stress lines, surprising considering the amount of pressure our jobs entailed. The only noticeable sign of wear were in her slightly calloused hands resulting from years of habitual wringing. I, on the other hand, seemed to be in a constant state of heightened dismay. The years of strain undoubtedly showed on my face, accompanied by an ever-present five o'clock shadow. Both our looks and our personalities balanced out in an ironic sort of way.

"My goal was not to 'alert the public.'" I stopped my frantic steps long enough to put air quotes around the common NYPD expression. "I needed to make him aware of the problem and assure him we can handle it. Therese, we're onto something really important."

My partner raised an eyebrow in annoyance. "Yes, you explained it me quite clearly just yesterday."

I leaned over the desk, tone dropping to a critical low. "We need to uncover whoever's behind this and shut them down. The fact that there might be a dealer lacing pot within a few blocks of that school scares the hell out of me."

"You don't have to convince me, Nathan. I know this is

huge." Therese was squeezing her hands together as she spoke. From years spent as her partner, I knew this meant she was uncomfortable and attempting to phrase her next words carefully. "Just . . . please be careful about bringing outside issues into work. And no," she cut in when I opened my mouth to interject, "I'm not saying that I believe that's the reason you picked up this case. It's just a gentle reminder of etiquette."

"Don't worry, Therese. I—"

A vibration in my pocket alerted me to an incoming call. I took the phone out and, upon seeing the contact was one of my many connections within the city, waved it towards Therese. She understood my meaning and raised a hand in farewell before turning back to her computer.

As I pressed accept and held the receiver to my ear, I mulled over Therese's words. Whatever she thought she knew about me, she was wrong. Even so, I couldn't help but hope that by working this case, we might be able to save someone else from going through what I did all those years ago.

4 CATHERINE

I slid down into an open seat, sighing in my acceptance of the grueling school week that faced me. After placing my bag against a leg of the desk, I took out my books and arranged them before me.

"She better not give us back that test we took last class," chatted Eve, sitting beside me and taking out her own text books. "I'm pretty sure I failed."

"You always say that and then you always do fine. I have absolutely no sympathy for you." My phone gave a final vibration when I turned it on silent before slipping it into my backpack. "Honestly, what's your average in this class?"

"A 90." Seeing my eye roll, she exclaimed, "But that's only half a percent above a B+!"

"Eve, I'm lucky if I get a B+ in this class."

The bell gave a final tone, effectively cutting off our

banter as the chemistry teacher strode to the front of the room.

"Good morning." Mrs. Kaydirman gave us her signature tight-lipped smile. She mindlessly pushed her spectacles to the bridge of her nose before uncapping a dry-erase marker. "Today we're beginning our new chapter: Introduction to Quantum Mechanics. You'll be having a test this Friday, so take plenty of notes." I groaned in chorus with the rest of the class. It was first period Monday morning and already the week was taking a turn for the worst.

"What?" One exclamation rose above the rest of our griping. Our teacher turned to the boy who spoke up. I identified his name as Francis. He was a stocky kid with bleach-blonde locks and a tanned complexion to match. His voice started forceful, but grew quieter now that her full attention was cast on him. "But we just had a test last class," he complained.

Mrs. Kaydirman stared at the boy. "Then you'll have perfected your studying technique and this exam should be easy." With countless years of teaching experience, she could be more than a little intimidating at times in the accuracy with which she read students. The way she held herself exuded confidence and a no-nonsense attitude. Francis, realizing he was fighting a losing battle, slid lower in his chair and glowered at the empty white-board.

The students around me began mumbling incoherently, but my mind was elsewhere. My mom had tried calling my dad this morning. I didn't know what she had been hoping for, but it wasn't the barrage of insults that met her on the other end. Familiar classmates and school work came as a semi-relief. At least I could rely on something to remain constant in my chaotic life.

Our teacher pulled down the projector screen to start a presentation. Contrary to the fact that class had only just started, I could tell it was going to be a long day. I turned my head to the right to check the clock.

A boy was staring directly at me. His forest green eyes met mine, causing me to silently panic. I quickly whipped my head back toward the projection screen. Who was that kid? And why was he staring at me? I half-heartedly attempted to concentrate on the diagrams of electron structures, but soon felt a tugging to steal another glance. Quickly, I flicked my eyes toward him again. He was staring at the projection, face blank and concentrated. Something in the back of my head reminded me that I should've been doing the same thing. But instead, I used the opportunity to get a better look.

He was tall, slightly muscular with broad shoulders. I noted a slight wave in his brown hair streaked with natural blonde. Following the curve of his jaw with my eyes, I couldn't deny that he was attractive. I couldn't remember seeing him before in class. But then again, I never really talked to anyone in class aside from Eve. Had I just not noticed him?

Scanning over his face and trying to make a match from my memories, I started when I realized he was looking directly at me. My gaze locked on his. I quickly turned back to the screen, concealing my face with my hair so he couldn't see me blushing. There was no reason for him to be looking at me. I wasn't doing anything strange or wearing something weird. Nothing that would lead him to stare at me like that. Why couldn't he just knock it off? It was distracting.

There was a tap on my shoulder. "What?" I whispered to Eve.

"Why were you looking at that guy?"

"I wasn't—" I rolled my eyes. "*He* was looking at *me*."

"No, I saw you. You were looking at him." My friend's eyes bulged in realization. "Wait a minute. You like him, don't you?"

"No!" I hissed at her. Mrs. Kaydirman turned in our direction and we quickly jotted a vague sentence onto our papers to appease her silent inquiry. When her back was turned to us once more, I repeated quietly, "No, I don't."

"Oh, you absolutely do." After a moment, Eve said, "Now he's looking at you." She painfully squeezed my arm in excitement as I jolted and pretended to be listening intently to the lesson. I could practically feel his eyes on me. There was no way he couldn't hear the blood pounding in my ears.

"It looked like he was staring at both of us." I murmured out of the side of my mouth.

"He's not staring at us. He's staring at *you*."

"Why would he be doing that? It's freaky."

"You know why." Eve slowly tilted her head toward mine. She hissed, "*Intuition*."

"Eve—"

"Don't even start. After class, you are staying behind and talking to him."

"Gimme a break, Eve, I think he's a junior!"

"So?"

"We're freshman!"

"And? Catherine, this is your chance! This is what you need. Go for it!"

"This is ridiculous. I don't even know his name."

"I'm sure you'll find out."

"Ladies." Mrs. Kaydirman's glasses were lowered to the edge of her nose, probing gaze aimed at Eve and me. "Would either of you be able to explain to us what a cation is?"

My face flushed and I realized we'd been caught. "I . . . no, sorry." Eve shook her head, expression apologetic.

"I recommend you pay attention to the lesson and keep the talking to a minimum." We nodded our understanding.

"Is there anyone else who would like to try? Samuel?"

The same boy we had been whispering about scanned his notes. He cleared his throat before saying, "It's a positive ion, isn't it?"

With one eyebrow raised in light surprise, Mrs. Kaydirman affirmed, "Correct." When she began discussing the differences between cations and anions, Eve scrawled something on the side of her paper before shoving it in my direction.

Now you know his name.

I thrust it back with a glare and attempted to concentrate on the lesson. We were already hopelessly behind. Being distracted by that boy, Samuel, wouldn't help my free-falling chemistry grade. Besides, we didn't have any idea who he was. He was probably just a creepy upperclassmen. Eve was making a big deal out of nothing.

When the bell finally rang, I folded two pages of scribbled notes into a binder as my mind swam with definitions and atom charges. Setting it on the edge of my desk, I turned to Eve to say something.

She was standing in front of me, face holding a strange expression. I opened my mouth to question it but she simply smiled before turning on her heels to begin walking slowly away. I moved to follow her and stopped when someone cleared their throat behind me. Biting my lip, I turned and found myself face-to-face with Samuel.

"Hi." His voice, deep and clear, was easily heard over the rest of the class' chatter. He raised his hand in a half-wave, giving me a small smile. "It's Catherine, right?"

"Right," I muttered, flicking my gaze toward the door. This was not happening. Not today. "Look, I have to—" At that moment, I heard a noise behind me. I turned just in time to see my binder crash to the floor. Papers scattered across the tiled surface, flying in every direction. As I dropped to my knees and began to gather my notes, I saw Eve racing toward the door. My mind put the pieces together. It was totally something she would do, a scene straight out of a movie. How old was the 'girl drops papers and boy helps pick them up' trick? I was going to *kill* her.

"Oh, wow," Samuel said, still standing before me and surveying the mess. "Do you need some help?"

"No." I crammed the crumpled papers back into my binder, ignoring the blush coloring my cheeks. "I've got it."

"Let me help you." Before I could object, he got down on both knees and started picking up what was left. He stood and held out his pile. "Here."

I grabbed it from his hands, shoving it back into my bag. "Thanks," I muttered. Looking toward the door again, I realized I couldn't get to it without going through Samuel first. Thanks to Eve, I was trapped.

"So," Samuel started, glancing from the floor to my face. "I'm Samuel."

"I know." After realizing what implications might be pulled from that remark, I quickly added, "I heard Mrs. Kaydirman say it." Heat flushed my face again. I was making a fool of myself. This was a horrible idea. I watched the students in the hall through the window in the door. My red-haired acquaintance was nowhere in sight. She was lucky for that.

"Oh." He shifted his weight from foot to foot. "You know, I've seen you around and stuff. Mostly in chemistry."

It was my turn to reply with, "Oh." I fiddled with the strap of my backpack, keeping my eyes on his. I tried to gauge what he was after, but got nothing from that pure orb of color. The scent of his fresh cologne caught my nose, a smoky mixture of cinnamon and fresh leather.

"Well, anyway, I was wondering if you . . . uh . . ." He paused. I broke eye-contact and continued scanning the hallway for Eve. As soon as I found her, I was saying some excuse and walking away. Then I was probably going to murder Eve for putting me in this situation in the first place.

Samuel suddenly closed his eyes, braced himself, and blurted, "Do you want to go out sometime?"

My frantic thoughts stopped. "Wait, what?"

Samuel's face fell. "I mean, if you don't want to, that's okay. I just thought…"

I stared wide-eyed at his despondent expression, his bright eyes examining the floor. In days prior, I would've denied him without hesitation. I had no idea who this kid was, and his first interaction with me was asking me on a date. Not exactly ideal circumstances. Didn't everyone say it was better to be friends first and move to dating status later?

But then I recalled Eve's whispered words: *This is your chance.* Okay, he was a little unconventional. Then again, there was nothing conventional about me, either. Besides, it was only a date. Maybe this was what I had been missing.

I took a deep breath and gathered my thoughts. Without giving myself the opportunity to second-guess, I managed, "Sure." Then, more forceful, "Yeah, okay."

Samuel nodded and his shoulders slumped with relief. A smile broke over his face. It was weird to think someone might be looking forward to spending time with me. Someone other than Eve, that is. I kind of liked it. "Well, how about after school today? At that cafe on 13th? We can meet in front of the library beforehand to walk together."

"Um … okay. Yeah."

"Great." He ran a hand through his hair then pointed down the hall. "I should probably get to class." I nodded, grinning wider now that the decision had been made. "See you later, Catherine."

I watched Samuel walk out of the classroom, carefully closing the door behind him. I let a few seconds pass before following. Shoving open the door, my eyes quickly found him amidst the many students. I watched him walk down the hall until he became lost in the crowd. He didn't seem too bad. It didn't hurt that he was cute, either. The more I thought about it, the more sure I became. Yes, this could work. Still straining to catch one last look, I didn't register Eve approaching and jumped when she spoke.

"Well? What's the date of the wedding?"

"Shut up."

5 NATHAN

"Detective Tawallis, you stated previously that the laced marijuana found actually contained a variety of substances. Can you elaborate on that?"

Squinting against the bright lights, I attempted to distinguish the face of the speaker concealed within the crowd. "Tests are still being done to isolate the exact chemicals added. They've been inconclusive thus far."

"Many theorize that marijuana will soon be legal across the United States. What do you have to say to those who believe that means it's safe?"

"That's a separate issue than what we're dealing with. Our main focus now is to keep our students safe." I leaned into the microphone extended from the podium to emphasize my next words. "By adding different chemicals or growing different strains of cannabis, the effects of the drug are altered. If people don't understand what they're taking, it can become extremely dangerous. Users who are used to pure marijuana may not be able to handle the additional kick that can come with it, potentially leading to an overdose. Young students who have only just started to experiment with drugs are especially vulnerable if they get their hands on the wrong material."

A small woman sporting a blonde bob raised a hand. "Hannah Moya, New York Times. Do you believe there is a single dealer behind all these cases of mixed marijuana?"

I swallowed. "Yes, I do. Informants have told us of an organized network being established. That, along with the close proximity of the overdoses, is what led us to that conclusion."

"Both students that overdosed attended the same high school. Is there a possibility someone within the school is a part of the operation?"

"We have begun to explore that theory. We cannot exclude the possibility that a student may work directly with a dealer and has become the supplier for their area. In this case, the supplier would be for the school itself. They don't understand the danger they're putting others and themselves in by selling these new mixes. If there is such a person, we encourage them to reveal themselves before anyone else gets hurt."

Multiple hands flew into the air. I motioned to one in the far left of the auditorium. "What is the NYPD doing to combat this issue?"

"We're doing our best to keep tabs on the situation and prevent it from growing further. Investigations are currently being conducted to gather as much information as possible on the lacings and the possibility of a supplier within the school."

"Is it true that you have a personal connection with this case, Detective Tawallis?"

I froze. My mind reeled, attempting to form a coherent thought, but none came.

It seemed like hours, but in reality only a few seconds of silence elapsed before Therese pushed past me to the front of the stage with clipboard in hand. Her tone left no room for exceptions. "That's enough questions for today. Thank you for your time."

The auditorium exploded in a cascade of shouts and camera flashes. Voices melded together, forming one roar. Making sure my livid temperament didn't show, I stepped down from the platform and moved toward the exit. It took all of my strength not to slam the door of the conference room once Therese had stepped inside. "How the *hell* did they find out about that?"

"I'm sure they're just pulling stuff out of the air," my

partner replied calmly. Although her voice exuded a cool composure, I could see her eyes gauging mine for weakness. "They're searching for a reaction out of you and think the story would make for an interesting read in the papers. They're not going to use it against you."

"There has got to be some regulations in place against that sort of shit. They can't just ask whatever they damn well please."

My partner held her hands out carefully toward me, signaling to me without words to calm down. Once I had steadied my breathing, she answered, "Honestly, Nathan, so what if they know? Now you've got some real motivation behind you. As long as you focus on *this* case, who the hell cares why you're doing it?"

There was an underlying accusation in her words that I didn't miss, but chose not to comment upon. I pushed my shoulders back, feeling my pulse slowly lower back to its normal rate. "You're right. Let's get this job done."

6 CATHERINE

What exactly was different about me, I couldn't quite put my finger on. The reflection staring back at me had eyes alight with energy, lips holding an ever-present smile. She looked nice, pretty even. She looked *alive*.

"Did you hear me?" Eve asked from her spot on the floor.

My reflection turned away with me as I drew my eyes to my friend. "What was that?"

A sigh accompanied Eve's exasperated eye-roll. She picked at the fibers woven into the plush carpet of my room. "I asked how the first date went! And don't leave anything out. I want all the juicy details."

I moved to perch on the foot of my bed, shifting so I could face her comfortably. The light blue mattress depressed slightly with my weight. "It was . . . alright, I guess." Eve sighed and crossed her arms, unconvinced. "Okay, okay," I relented, biting my lip. "It was really good."

"I knew it! What was he like? I know absolutely nothing about this guy."

"I mean, he's really nice. And funny." I swung my legs back and forth, letting the tips of my toes brush the top fibers of the carpet. "I've got to be honest, Eve, at first I was having a lot of doubts about this whole thing. But he seems like a good guy."

Eve smiled and pumped her fists. "I could just tell that this was gonna work out! See, you gotta listen to my intuition! Okay, so first date done. Where are you two going next?"

"We're seeing a Broadway show this weekend."

With an exaggerated gasp, Eve sat back on her hands, mouth gaping. "He bought you tickets to a Broadway show on your *second date?*"

I had been surprised too when he texted me the news a day after our first date. He was taking some pretty big leaps forward. A hint of pride edged my voice as I explained, "He said he found a deal on tickets."

"Even cheap tickets are going to be at least $80 each! He must be really into you. Either that or he has some sort of secret wealth." Eve looked thoughtful before adding, "Both of which are very good options."

I continued to swing my legs back and forth, heels

tapping. "Yeah, I guess you're right."

Eve smiled, then leapt up to wrap her arms around me. Her voice was muffled slightly in my shoulder. "I'm proud of you, Catherine." I couldn't help but smile at the happiness in my friend's voice. "Look what happens when you take a leap of faith!" She stepped back and placed a hand on her hip. "I also think someone deserves a thank-you for making this happen?"

I tipped my head in acknowledgement. "Where would I be without my BFF? I wish there was some way I could repay you."

"Permission to live vicariously through your love-life will be enough." We shared a laugh and, for the first time in longer than I could remember, I felt truly happy. This was going better than I ever could've imagined.

7 FRANK

Rivers closed the door behind him, pulling the hood up on his jacket as he did so. The empty space in my pocket where the stack of cash had been felt acutely vacant. As risky as it was carrying around large sums of cash, it assured me that these transactions couldn't be tracked. My employees were all aware of the risk that came with the job and I had to do everything in my power to keep that risk to a minimum. Using a credit card that could be easily tracked was a beginner's mistake. I was in no way new to this line of work.

Just as I was about to turn away from the door, it flew open again. "Ah," I commented, slow-clapping a sarcastic introduction. "It's my Scavenger."

The kid had a beaming look on his face that was only slightly dampened by the use of his nickname. "It's been set up," he explained. "Everything is ready."

I crossed the room to sit behind the oak desk positioned to the right of the doorway. A stack of forms restricting my view was quickly pushed aside so I could meet McGee's eyes. "Feeling more confident about the new target, I see."

He shrugged. "She fell for it without question. I'll admit, she's a little different than the usual clientele, but she has potential."

"You think you're ready for the Usher?"

"Yeah. Just give me one now and I'll come back for more when she's ready." I grabbed a premade joint from one of my desk drawers and handed it to him. He pocketed it in one swift motion, the weight of what he was carrying lost after years of contact.

"Now don't get it mixed up with the others you have. You'll be completely over the edge after a few pulls."

McGee gave me a withering look. "You know I don't use."

"Just clarifying in case you have a change of heart. Remember our deal." My eyes scanned his expression while I cracked the knuckles in both my hands. First the right one, then the left. It was a small and effective show of power I used on occasion. Tricks of the trade. "Hook the girl or pay up."

"Of course." He turned to leave.

Glancing down at the date on my watch, I called to his

retreating figure, "Oh, and have fun on Monday, Scavenger." The kid stiffened. "It's the first of the month, and you know what that means."

His knuckles grew white against the door handle. "You know, I think I'd prefer if you used my real name."

I rolled my eyes, drawing out each syllable. "As you wish, *Samuel*."

8 CATHERINE

"So, how did you like it?"

Glancing down at my hand wrapped in his, I replied, "It was actually really cool. I have no idea how they did that thing with the chandelier. I totally get why people obsess over those shows."

Samuel moved closer to me and I didn't pull away. "Pretty good idea to come here, huh?"

"Yeah," I said. After thinking for a moment, I nuzzled closer to him. "Thank you for taking me."

Samuel gave me a wide smile. "The pleasure was all mine." Over the few days we had been together, I felt surprisingly comfortable around him. There was a mutual confidence between us that allowed us to be open and honest about everything. I could tell him anything, and he would do the same. That was something I felt like I couldn't do with anyone else aside from maybe Eve. Not even in my own home.

We continued strolling through the theater district, two among countless others in awe of the performance they just witnessed. Every bright and colorful billboard we passed made me wonder what secrets and surprises each show contained. I had heard people talk about Broadway shows before, but never had the opportunity to experience them first hand. I felt like I had been let in on a secret.

The murmurings of the city reached our ears, far-off car horns and music echoing through the streets. Night had fallen, but we still had plenty of light to see by cast from streetlights and shops. It was one of those rare times when you simply breathe in the moment, savoring each passing second so it becomes burned into your memory. I took in the noise, the lights; and the boy walking beside me.

Samuel swung our clasped hands back and forth between us freely. "So, I take it your first show was a success?"

"Absolutely. I've always wanted to go, but never could." I paused and lowered my eyes. It would've been fine to cut the comment off at that, but I felt comfortable enough to go on. "Even when my mom and dad were still together, we never had enough cash coming in to do something like that. And there's definitely no way now, after — everything." Samuel made a small noise: not pity, but understanding. A wave of relief swept over me. He understood. More confident now, I added, "Speaking of home, do you think we could go to your place sometime next week to study for Chem? We have that test coming up and I could use a study partner."

Samuel's sure steps faltered for a moment, so slight I might have imagined it. "Oh," he responded. "I'm sure you'd prefer the library. My house is . . . loud."

He hadn't said it outright, but the tone of his voice let me know his home-life wasn't perfect either. We were in the same position. There was something comforting in knowing that someone was going through a similar situation. I let it drop, knowing I would want him to do the same if he had asked.

A few seconds passed where the only sound to be heard was our shoes slapping the pavement. Samuel broke the silence, voice cool and confident once again. "But I would love to study with you somewhere else."

"Okay. The library would work." Pushing a piece of hair behind one ear with my free hand, I chuckled, "Come to think of it, my house probably wouldn't be a great option either. It's pretty small. And old." There was also the problem of my mom not knowing about Samuel. Something made me not want to let her know about him just yet. It was a little personal secret I had the ability to keep, something I had control over. I would let her know when I was ready. Lucky for me, she was out tonight so I wouldn't have to worry about her prying eyes when I got home. But I knew I couldn't put it off forever.

"I'm sure it's great." Unlinking his hand from mine, he moved to drape it over my shoulders. I couldn't help but smile as his warm embrace pushed away the evening chill. This dating thing wasn't turning out to be so bad. I couldn't remember the last time I felt this comfortable around someone. We stayed in content quiet the rest of the walk.

When we made the final turn onto my street, I directed him to my house. Small abodes lined the street on either side, two impenetrable walls of windows and doors. The entrance to my own was situated at the top of a small flight of stairs. It was quaint and squarely shaped, not unlike the others on the street. The only truly distinguishing factor was the small bronze number 72 nailed slightly crooked to the door.

Samuel led me to the top of the stairs dimly lit by the weak, yellow porch-light. Once we were both standing in front of the door, I said softly, "I told you it wasn't much."

He took in the small windows, faded blinds and paint chipping slightly off the door. "Oh, come on. It's great." Samuel gestured to the homes on either side. "It's so great they made a thousand others just like it."

I laughed. "Well, that's very kind of you. Although I'm not sure I would agree." I shyly met his eyes, keenly aware of our hands still entwined.

We stood in silence. I felt expectant for something, but I wasn't sure what. Then Samuel looked toward the empty street. "I probably should be heading back," he said.

"Right." After a final squeeze, he let go and began walking down the steps. I called out to his retreating figure, "See you tomorrow?"

Samuel stopped where he was. When he turned around, he was grinning from ear to ear. "Of course," he replied.

9 NATHAN

I shoved the final pin into the cork board before stepping back to admire my work. The map stretched from one side of the office to the other, a Picasso-style arrangement of streets and buildings. Plucking a red marker from a small cup holding a variety of writing utensils, I carefully traced the outline of the high school. "Almost done," I announced, capping the marker and placing it back in its rightful spot.

Therese stood with crossed arms in front of my desk. "Looks great," she said, eyes roaming the surface of the paper. "Though I'm not exactly sure what it is."

I removed a designated stack of photos and note cards from my back pocket. When I finished pinning them up, I finally saw the realized image I had pictured in my mind. "I have just completed a full layout of our current case, condensed for our convenient viewing into one bulletin board."

My partner nodded and took in the new additions. "Not bad. Not very useful, either, but not bad."

"I'm a visual person." I pointed to various markings scattered across the thick paper. "See these symbols? I've marked every drug-related-infraction over the last five years that occurred within these blocks. It's helping me narrow down locations and times to find the patterns." My arms waved wide to encompass the whole board. "If we use this correctly, we might be able to isolate the person we're looking for. Maybe even get to the distributor."

Therese gestured a hand at me. "Put on the brakes, Nathan. Even if we do end up catching someone, chances are slim to none they're going to spill about their source. These people make pacts bound in blood." It seemed to be more and more often that Therese was pulling me back down to reality, whether from emotional peaks or from getting ahead of myself. My own brashness was beginning to wear on my nerves.

"I'm not just going out on a limb. I've done research. The location and frequency of these offenses lead me to believe that there is a large operation in very close proximity to that school. If there's an operation, there's going to be someone there running it."

My partner leaned against my desk, hands clasped tightly in front of her. "And I'm assuming you want us to be the ones who break the case open?"

"We're the ones heading this thing. We'll get there."

She gave me one last look before pointing to a badly drawn skull inked onto the map. "What's this symbol for?"

I stopped. Much as I tried, I couldn't keep the waver out of my voice. "That means there was a death involving contraband of some kind."

Therese bit her lip. After a second's pause, she squinted at the drawing. "You should choose a new symbol. Your art skills suck."

She was lightening the mood, skirting around the name in the forefront of both our minds. "Okay, sure," I said, choosing to play along. "Do you have any other witty suggestions?"

My partner glanced down at the watch encircling her left wrist. "Nah. I think that covers it. Keep me updated?"

"Mmhm," I murmured, but my attention was already back on the map. The person causing all this was concealed out there somewhere amidst the skyscrapers. It was only a matter of time before I tore down their facade.

10 SAMUEL

I checked the date on my phone again. Unwilling to heed to my desire for it to say otherwise, it continued to read *Monday, May 1*. Every month I had the same internal argument. Every month I tried to convince myself to visit another day or to just skip coming altogether. Every month I failed.

My ears caught each sound on the deadly silent subway, seats lined with adults absorbed in the glow of their cell phones. One could spot a teenager or two in the mix, still riding on the short-lasting thrill of being able to travel without a parent's watchful gaze. Track rumbled underneath the car and I lost myself in the white sound. It was easier to ignore the destination awaiting me.

It seemed like only seconds had passed before the screeching of brakes could be heard piercing through the noise. The view from the window showed blurred images slowly coming into clarity as the car began to decrease its speed. I grabbed my backpack and the two bags of groceries that sat between my feet, gripping the vertical metal pole tightly with the other hand. The passengers around me silently gathered their things, preparing to disembark. When the doors slid open with a hiss, I stood back and allowed others to pass before slowly shuffling off the tram. Keeping my head down was difficult while I attempted to navigate through the crowd. There wasn't a large chance I would be recognized, but one could never be too safe in such a crowded city.

I followed the passengers carefully, melding seamlessly into the flow of people. A sign several hundred feet away pointed toward an entrance that led up to ground level. The crowd swept me towards it and I allowed them. Bright rays of sunlight bore down, causing me to blink rapidly as my eyes adjusted. Light reflected off the metal exteriors of the buildings and into my eyes. Putting up one hand to block their glare, I avoided the group of people huddled around the map, then turned left. The walk to the neighborhood seemed shorter than usual. It always did. My heart dropped with the conditions of my surroundings. Shiny fronts of businesses turned to rickety houses with boarded windows. Loud music and chatter faded to an empty quiet.

The shopping bags dug into my palms and I shifted them carefully as I scanned the streets for any potential trouble. My feet stopped suddenly, seemingly of their own accord. I had arrived.

A cat cried out from an indistinguishable spot nearby as I forced myself to step onto the narrow walkway. At first I attempted to avoid the cracks in the cement, but soon became overwhelmed by the overlaying, web-like fractures. The door's maroon paint was hopelessly chipped, an especially marred area at level with my feet. It had one circular window imbedded into the center of its frame. Although it was foggy beyond usage, the position of the reflective glass in the doorframe conjured images of a foreboding cyclops, imperfections in the wood serving as fangs.

Stepping onto the porch, I raised my hand to ring the bell. A sudden thought dawned on me and I chose instead to pull the key from my pocket. I wouldn't want to wake them if they were sleeping. If that were the case, I might be able to get through the visit without having to exchange words with them. The doorknob required a bit more effort than expected to turn and the key stuck before I was able to force it out. Taking a deep breath, I pushed open the door.

The heavy stench of stale beer and foot-odor hit me like a wall. A rough cough was forced from my throat as my stomach turned. Covering my face with the back of one hand, I stepped over the threshold before closing the door behind me.

Few, if any, changes had been made to the room since the last time I stepped foot inside. A television lit up the room in a blue glow, the drawn curtains preventing any natural light from entering. The screen was currently showing one of the countless soap operas I'd seen it tuned to in months past. A shapeless form covered by a thin blanket stretched across the lumpy, stained couch.

It wasn't moving.

I moved to kneel beside the ratty piece of furniture, pulling the grocery bags behind me. I pushed a stack of empty beer cans off a cushion before placing my full attention on the figure.

"Hey," I whispered. There was no response. Shaking what I thought was a shoulder, I tried again. "Hey, can you hear me?" Still nothing. I began frantically tapping as my heart began to race. "Wake up, wake—"

I released a sigh of relief when a moan came from within the folds of the blanket. A mop of matted hair sat up before a pale, shaking hand shoved it aside to reveal a familiar face. Her sunken eyes met mine as the corners of her lips were forced upward into what might've been a smile years ago.

"Why," slurred my mother, "if it isn't Sammy."

Her sticky, alcohol-scented breath wafted over my face. "Hi, Mom." Dodging her bony hand as it moved to grab my arm, I lifted up the bags. "Look, I bought more groceries for you."

"What a good boy," she said as she reached up her arms. Her back gave a sickening crack. The movement revealed circular, yellow splotches staining the underarms of her shirt. "Sammy takes care of his mother."

I wanted to shout at her, *But do you ever take care of me? Do you ever ask where I go, where I've been? Are you ever not so wasted that you even spare me a second thought?* I wanted to scream so many things at her I kept in the darkest part of my mind.

But instead I walked to the fridge and settled for, "Yeah, I do." I removed anything empty or expired from its shelves. All of it was food I had previously purchased, most of it untouched. This included a full carton of milk which, upon my checking, exuded a putrid stench. I replaced them with a block of cheese, margarine, fresh milk and a few other necessities taken from the shopping bag. I was aware there was a large chance I would find them untouched at the time of my next visit. Continuing with my monthly tasks, I placed other various goods on the laminate countertop. Once the shopping bags were empty, I gathered up the garbage that littered most available surfaces and shoved it into the bags to conserve waste.

"Are you still going to school?" drawled my mother from her position on the couch.

"Yes." *I'm not becoming a dropout. I'm not like you.*

She gave a snort. "Can't be sure, ya know, since you're never home anymore."

Maybe if you gave me a proper home to live in, I would stay.

I shoved another crushed soda can into the quickly filling grocery bag.

"Who are you staying with now?"

It genuinely surprised me that she was sober enough to ask such a question. "Jim," I lied easily.

There was a pause, before, "I thought you were with Evan."

I had given her a different name than the last time. Even though I realized my mistake, I knew she would never push the point. "Nope. It was Jim."

"Huh." Her voice implied that her mind had already moved on. That was how our usual conversations progressed: floating from topic to pointless topic.

I finished placing the last scraps inside and tied the bag shut. "Okay," I said. "I've got to go." Giving the couch a wide berth, I made a bee-line for the door. "I'll see you later." My mother muttered her response, head already back under the covers. I was a few steps away from the exit when I heard the floorboards creak behind me.

My father had appeared in the doorframe of the bedroom. Shadows darkened the details of his face, but it was apparent that his gut had extended further since last month. His alcohol-fogged gaze was glassy and vague.

"Babe," he grunted to the blanketed figure, waving a finger at me. "Who's that kid?"

I slammed the door behind me before taking off down the sidewalk. Stopping at the first trash can I saw, I threw open the lid and stuffed the overflowing bags inside. My nails bit into my palms as I struggled against the blood roaring in my ears, but I wasn't strong enough to keep the tears from escaping my eyes.

11 CATHERINE

I watched Eve extract another tube from the bag. This one was slightly smaller than the last one. It had thin, spidery font engraved on the front, but too much of it was scratched off for me to read. She waved it at me, saying, "This is mascara. Do you at least know what that is?"

"I think so." My face felt weird when I moved, the liquid foundation creating a strange sensation on my skin. It felt lighter than face-paint but similar in texture. "That's what you put around your eyes, right?"

"*No!* That's eye-liner!" Eve placed her head in her hands and groaned, "Catherine, you are impossible to work with. You're so clueless, I should be getting paid to help you with this."

"I never officially asked for your help. You were the one who said I needed to 'update my look' for Samuel. And might

I remind you, I do wear some makeup."

"You wear powder foundation and blush. That barely counts. What about the highlight, the bronzer, the eye-shadow, *the contour?*"

I leaned back on the stool, eyes rolling. "I don't know what half of those words even mean."

"But you will!" Unscrewing the top, she waved the rounded brush end at me. "Now open your eyes and look up." I obliged and Eve began applying the black liquid to my eyelashes.

"I really don't think this is necessary." I quickly discovered the new struggle of attempting to keep my head still and talking simultaneously. "Samuel seemed perfectly fine with how I looked."

"I'm not changing how you look." She switched hands to work on my other eye. "I'm simply accentuating your best features so they stand out."

"You sound like a make-up saleswoman."

Eve ignored me, concentrating with laser-like focus. Eventually, she sat back and seemed satisfied. "There. Take a look in the mirror."

I spun the stool around, afraid to turn my head lest I smear her work. The reflection's eyebrows raised with my own. My eyes seemed larger than usual, but not necessarily in a bad way. My skin definitely looked smoother and held a noticeable glow. I tilted my head from side to side to see it from all angles.

"Well?" Eve questioned.

"It's not . . . bad."

My friend pumped her fists in the air, triumphant. "That's as close as I'm going get to approval! You don't have to wear it all the time if you don't want to, but for dates and—" She winked at me. "—special occasions it can come in handy." She held out a hand. "That'll be $20 for my hard work."

"Eve."

"Kidding!"

There was a knock on my bedroom door. "Do you girls mind if I pop in for a moment?"

"It's fine, Mom," I called.

The door swung wide, revealing the smiling face of my mother. Her naturally straight hair was pulled back into a loose bun, stray pieces tucked behind her ears. She took in the brushes, palettes and bottles spread across my dresser. "Now, what are you two up to?"

"I'm giving your daughter a make-over, Mrs. Linnel," Eve explained, holding the foundation brush with the same amount of respect a knight would grip his sword with.

"I've told you before, Eve, it's perfectly acceptable to call me Claire." My mother gave me a smile. "And you look wonderful."

"I know, right?" My friend gave me a knowing look. "She needs to look her best for Samuel." I inwardly cringed, realizing what that simple statement had done.

My mother let out a gasp, more of delight and surprise than anger. "Wait, what? Who's this Samuel?"

"He's Catherine's boyfriend. He's a junior," piped Eve, then let out a muffled cry when I kicked her shin.

"A junior? Why did you not mention this sooner, Catherine?"

Shrugging, I said in what I hoped was an innocent tone, "I was going to tell you eventually. Besides, there's not much to know about it." It was the truth. Well, it was *part* of the truth.

"Catherine Linnel, you are going to tell me about this boy."

"Samuel's fine, Mom. We've only been dating a week."

"*A week?* That's seven days I've been kept completely in the dark about this!" She crossed her arms and leaned into one side of the doorframe. "This boy is taking my only daughter out into the city. I want you to tell me who this boy is and I'm not leaving until that happens." Eve smirked at me, watching the conversation progress. Although she didn't know I hadn't told my mom about Samuel, she was definitely enjoying my awkwardness. The second kick I threw in her direction was narrowly avoided.

"Well, our only class together is chemistry. He's been pretty nice."

"What does he do outside of school?"

"He . . . uh . . ." I wasn't actually sure. "I'm sure he does stuff, it just hasn't come up when we've talked."

"Does he play a sport?"

I struggled to come up with a neutral response. ". . . Probably."

My mother stared at me fixedly. Her expression exuded wariness with a hint of disappointment. "Sounds like you don't know much about this kid."

I had come to that same realization, but I wasn't planning on telling her that. "I know plenty about him! He's a good person, I can tell." I made a mental note to ask him some more questions the next time I saw him. Not for my sake, but just to appease her.

There was a moment of silence before my mother said, "Is that really it?"

Eve jumped in and took over, words tumbling out of her mouth as fast as she could think of them. "Well, we don't have any classes with him besides that one and the whole thing was really quite unexpected. I've seen them together and they're just too cute. None of my inner-warning-alarms go off or anything. Don't worry, Mrs.—" She backtracked, realizing her error, "Don't worry, Claire. I'm looking out for Catherine."

Eve's hurried explanation did nothing to change the look on my mother's face. It was still present when she replied, "Just promise me you'll be careful, Catherine. Promise me you won't do anything you'll regret."

"*Okay*, Mom." It must've been obvious that I was trying to get her to leave but I was quickly running out of patience. "Samuel's fine. Everything's fine. He's a good person, I know he is."

12 THE BOY, AGE 12

"We're here."

Frank pulled the boy to a stop in front of the apartment. While he rummaged in his pocket for the key, the boy pointed to the label on the off-white door.

"Number seven."

Glancing up, Frank nodded. "Yeah, apartment seven."

"Isn't seven a lucky number?"

"It's supposed to be," Frank muttered, sticking the key into the doorknob. "But that's a load of crap."

Unphased by Frank's language, the boy continued, "We should name this place 'Lucky Seven.'"

"Like you're calling my other apartment 'Robinson' because it's 42?" Frank laughed and pushed the door open. "There's nothing lucky about this place, Sammy." The boy shrugged, having been well-acquainted with Frank's sense of humor. It had unnerved him at first, but by now he was used to it.

The boy took in the cramped space. Boxes were lined from floor to ceiling, pressed against every wall and into every crevice. Thick blinds covering the windows blocked the view from the outside world. The air held a pungent odor that the boy didn't recognize, tart with a touch of sweet.

An open box filled with small bags caught his eye. "What's that?"

"That's the snow." Frank took his arm, pulling him away. "Don't go touching that stuff, it's not for playing."

"Snow? Wouldn't it have to be kept cold or something?"

"This is a different kind of snow." Frank paused to stare at the boy. He seemed to be thinking. "How old are you now?"

"Twelve and a half."

After a second's thought, Frank shrugged. "I guess you're old enough. What the hell do I know about raising kids?" He gestured the boy over to a small box on the ground. After brushing it off, he gestured for him to sit. Frank took a seat across from him and looked the boy over carefully. "Do you have any idea what I do for a living?"

The boy glanced around what Frank had told him was a storage space. Some of the boxes were open, some were closed. A few had tags with strange languages on them that he couldn't read. "I know you give me assignments and have me deliver a bunch of packages to people."

"You really have no idea?"

Scrunching his eyebrows together in thought, the boy said, "Do you run a post-office?"

"No, not a post-office." Frank dropped his head. "Oh, God, how do I explain this?" He glanced up at the boy's expectant, if somewhat confused, expression. Putting his hands out, Frank began slowly, "Alright. Listen, kid. My job is to deliver stuff for people that they use for — fun."

"Like toys and stuff?"

"No, not toys. More like recreational stuff. It helps people relax and makes them feel better."

"So, medicine?"

"No . . ." Seeing there was no way around the fact, Frank relented, "I sell drugs."

"Some people call medicine drugs." The boy straightened as something clicked in his mind. "Wait, do you mean ... *those* kind of drugs?"

"Yeah, probably."

"But . . ." He began folding a flap of the box nervously. "Those are really dangerous."

Frank blinked, thinking hard. "Well, I mean — it depends how they use them."

The boy's voice was quiet. "I've heard people die from

them."

"No! I mean — yes, sometimes, but not if you know what you're doing. If you try the hard stuff first, then it gets dangerous. But there are ways around it. Like this." Gesturing to a smaller box off to the side, he explained, "That's a strain I've cultivated called Usher. It helps people get used to it before they use something that's too strong. So they don't die. Does that make sense?"

Biting his lip, the boy gave no response. The flap went up and down, up and down.

"Listen, Samuel." Frank leaned toward the boy and attempted to make his voice sincere. If only he could break through to him and make him understand. What he was doing wasn't bad. It was just business. "If they don't get it from us, they'll get it from someone else. We might as well make some sorta profit. We're not holding a gun to their head or forcing them to buy. It's their choice. Besides, we're not killing anyone. They do that to themselves."

There was a pause before the boy relented, "Okay, I guess."

Feeling he had filled his obligation as a guardian, Frank stood and began to lead the boy back to the door. "You just do your job and I'll worry about mine, kid. You're doing great so far. Hell, maybe one day I'll even make you my official partner."

The boy agreed, wondering what his new assignment would be if he became Frank's partner.

13 SAMUEL

"Name the orbital layers in the third quantum level of an atom."

"Um . . ." I glanced away from the road to see Catherine's eyes scrunched in concentration. "S, p and d."

"And how many electrons does each level contain?"

"2, 6 and 10."

I nodded my affirmation. My hands tightly clutched the armrest when the bus drove over a divot in the spotty pavement. "You're totally prepared. You've got nothing to worry about."

"I really hope you're right. This test is basically life or death for my chem grade." Her head turned back toward the window. There wasn't much to see, the sun having set over an hour ago. "So, where are we going exactly?"

I shrugged. "I don't know."

Catherine raised a brow. "What do you mean 'you don't know?' We've been on this bus for almost thirty minutes. *Please* tell me you know where we are."

"Maybe I mean I can't tell you."

"Oh." Her face brightened as she entertained the prospect. "You mean it's a surprise."

"I'm not distinctly confirming or denying that theory. But it's a possibility."

"Okay," Catherine laughed. "I'll be surprised. I trust you."

A mistake. I kept my gaze turned away from hers so she couldn't see the betrayal hiding behind my eyes. She probably wouldn't be able to tell even if I did make eye-contact. I had been doing this for months now. No one could ever tell.

I listened to the quiet music being piped in through the speakers, allowing it to fill the silence so I didn't have to. The bus was quiet. Catherine and I were alone aside from one man sitting in the second to last row. He had the demeanor of an office worker, tired eyes and hunched shoulders.

The bus pulled onto an exit for a bridge and onto a thinner road. Catherine still didn't say anything, but I saw the confusion written on her face. She had no idea where we were going. The ride was vividly burned into my mind after frequent visits, even though I hadn't traversed it in years. The last time I drove this way, I was living a different life.

Time passed slowly. We had exhausted small-talk and hadn't exchanged words in quite a while. After I became aware of an uncharacteristically long silence on Catherine's end, I noticed her nodding off beside me. It was a matter of minutes before her head leaned against my shoulder. A smirk broke over my face. I was getting the hang of this 'caring boyfriend' facade. When Catherine's breathing became soft and even, I shifted to get a better look at the girl Frank had randomly plucked from the crowd.

She was pretty in a plain sort of way; smooth features, a round nose and high cheek bones with pale rose lips. A black cascade of hair holding a slight wave partially concealed her face, revealing only one eye blanketed with thick lashes. In sleep, she seemed peaceful. Her mouth turned slightly upward as if she were recalling a happy memory during her slumber.

I found myself smiling down at her, wondering what she was dreaming about.

Shaking my head sharply, I forced my gaze away from her and pinched the back of my hand. I wouldn't let myself go soft. I couldn't forget what I was here for. This girl was chosen for a purpose. That purpose was not for love. She was just another client.

Reaching my hand into my pocket, I checked to make sure it was still there. It was.

The bus began to slow down and, as if on cue, Catherine lifted her head from my shoulder. "Are we here?" she asked sleepily. Her voice lilted upwards the way it sometimes does when one speaks but half of the brain isn't fully awake.

"I think so." I pushed a piece of hair out of her face and behind her ear. "Now, I want you to keep your eyes closed as we get off the bus."

"What? Samuel, I'm going to walk into something."

"You don't have to worry, I'll guide you. Promise me you will?"

The bus came to a complete stop and the doors pulled open. The man at the back of the bus shut his briefcase and quickly disembarked. Catherine looked at me, then sighed in acceptance and shut her eyes. "Okay. But if I fall, it's your fault."

"I won't let you fall. Now hold onto me. We have some steps to get down first." Her hands found mine and I carefully led her down the stairs. Her grip became tighter with each passing step. "Last one and . . . you're good. We just have a little farther to go. You doing okay?"

"Yeah, I guess." Uncertain interest filled her tone.

"Don't worry, we're almost there. Let me lead you the rest of the way."

Our hands remained entwined as I patiently pulled her down the pathway. Anyone watching would've given us a strange look, but luckily there was no one in sight. Just as I'd hoped.

We reached the edge of the grass and I placed her hands on the railing surrounding the area. "Okay, you can open your eyes now."

Catherine obliged, still on edge. She blinked in the waning light as her eyes adjusted. When the view came into clarity, she gasped, "Samuel — it's beautiful."

We were standing at the edge of a clearing overlooking the city. Buildings rose before us like jagged teeth along the shoreline. A red hue shrouded the city, rays of sun twinkling off the tallest of the buildings. It seemed like something out of a painting; we could appreciate the beauty of New York without the unflattering noises or smells that so often accompanied it.

Catherine shook her head in wonder, subconsciously winding the fingers of her left hand into my right. "I never knew the city could be so beautiful."

"It's sometimes good to take a step back," I said without thinking. Letting out a laugh, I explained, "My mom used to say that every time she took my family here. We used to have family picnics right in this courtyard. She didn't really enjoy living in New York, but out here it was somehow different. Things used to be so different . . ." I trailed off as the memory faded away.

Catherine studied my expression carefully. She must have read the underlying pain, but let it pass. "Where is 'here,' exactly?"

"Weehawken."

It took a few seconds for the name to resurface the memory. "Hey . . ." She turned to me slowly, pursing her lips thoughtfully. "Isn't this the place where that guy was shot?"

"Alexander Hamilton?"

"Yeah!"

"'That guy,'" I remarked, laughing at her choice of words. "I think I know what musical we should see next."

"Yeah, good luck getting tickets. You're not getting some crazy deal for that show."

I shrugged. "You'd be surprised. I have connections."

Catherine stepped closer to me, fly-away hairs tickling the side of my neck. "Thank you for bringing me here."

"You're very welcome." When the conversation paused, I knew it was time.

"Hey," I started, but something made me stop. My fingers wrapped around it in my pocket and prepared to pull it out.

Straightening, Catherine asked, "What?"

"I have a question for you." It had been so easy with the others I had worked with. *Do you want to try this? Have you ever smoked pot before? I know what would make this night even better.*

Any one of those phrases would direct the conversation back where it needed to be.

But something wouldn't let me pull the joint out of my pocket.

"What's your question?" she said.

I turned to face her. "I . . ." *Damn it*, what was wrong with me? I needed to pull myself together. My brain seemed stuck, like a broken recording spinning on the same line of song. "I wanted to know if . . ."

Catherine looked at me, expectancy twinkling in her eyes.

Mind gone blank, I blurted, "I wanted to know if you'd go to prom with me." As I inwardly cursed myself furiously, Catherine let out a gasp of delight.

"Of course I will!" She threw her arms around me and, although the anger was still burning fierce, it dulled for a single moment at her touch.

I hesitated, but let myself grip her back. *This is not real*, I reminded myself. *You do not love her. She is nothing to you.* Even as my inner thoughts rebelled, I could feel her warmth against me. She rested underneath my chin, head nestled comfortably against my chest. I closed my eyes and tried to calm the warring ocean of emotions filling my head.

As she pulled away, Catherine let out a giggle. "Eve is going to be pissed . . ." I couldn't help but raise a questioning eyebrow. "My friend, Eve. She had a bet that you would do a promposal with some cheesy sign or something. I thought you would do something less over the top." Catherine waved outward toward the city, grinning ear to ear. "Something exactly like this."

The phrase tugged at something nestled in the back of my mind. I wrapped my arm around her, the unsmoked joint feeling like it was on fire in my pocket.

14 THE BOY, AGE 11

"Something exactly like this is what I'm talking about, Frank!" The boy pressed himself closer against the wall to catch the woman's words. His ear was flush with the surface's chipped paint. "You never think before you act, you just make impulsive decisions out of nowhere—"

"Well, Nickie, what the hell was I supposed to do? Let him go back to that house? The first time I found him he was wandering the streets and begging for food. Next he had a cut on his head he told me came from his father. This time there are bruises all over his arms—"

"That's not my problem, and it's not yours either!" Something slammed down onto a table. "The government has people to take care of stuff like this. You're the last person I'd expect to suddenly become a bleeding-heart." The boy's hands rubbed up and down his arms nervously as he listened. They throbbed in beat with his elevated heart rate. Frank and the woman had been arguing ever since he and Frank arrived. Their voices grew louder with each passing remark. The woman in particular seemed especially worked up.

"I can't believe you would ask me to take a random kid into my house," she exclaimed. "I don't even know his name!"

"His name is Samuel and it would only be temporary. I'm going to try to find a better place for him. But for now, I can't let him go back to that house."

"Actually, Frank, you can. You can send him home just like you did—"

"Don't you dare bring him back into it. He was a bad influence on you, I was doing you a favor."

"Dammit, I loved him! Not that you give a shit." There was a pause before Nickie continued in what could only be described as a growl, "I know you're not taking this kid in out of the goodness of your heart. Everything you do has some deeper, darker motive. What are you planning to do with him, huh? *What's going on in your head?*"

"I don't want you to argue about me." Frank and Nickie hadn't heard the door open or the boy step inside, but his voice cut through their shouts. Their faces were both flushed from yelling. Nickie's hair with tips dyed green were fanned around her face. She stared at him, eyes wide with emotion. The boy understood that this argument was his fault. For some reason, he seemed to cause a lot of people to fight. After Frank had been so nice, buying him pizza and giving him money, he couldn't watch them argue on account of him. "I think I'll go home now."

The boy moved toward the door but a hand reached out to grip his upper arm. "Wait." He looked into the woman's face. Her gaze traveled to the partially healed wound crossing his forehead and then to meet his eyes. Her expression was torn, teeth biting deep into the flesh of her lower lip. They stayed like that for seconds on end while her mind worked. What was going on inside her head, the boy couldn't tell. Her expression slowly shifted from dark anger to pained resignation. She finally whispered, "I think I have an extra room you can stay in." Her hazel eyes never left his.

"That's alright. I can go home."

"Nonsense." Her voice was calming now, compassionate, even. Nickie carefully took his hand and led him deeper into the house. Her hand moved from his arm to rest protectively on his shoulder. "I'll take care of you, clean you up and all. At least for a little while."

Frank began, "Thank you—"

"Don't," Nickie snapped, grip tightening on the boy. "I'm not doing this for you." She led him away, refusing to look at her brother. Once it was clear she wasn't coming back, Frank left the house without another word.

15 FRANK

The front door slammed. I jumped and lifted my weary eyes away from the paperwork spread on the table before me. Shuffling footsteps accompanied the slumped figure of McGee as made his way into the kitchen of the small apartment. His aura rapidly shifted into one of aggression when he saw me seated at the table. "What are you doing here?" he demanded.

Giving a note of annoyance, I shoved my documents unceremoniously into one haphazard pile. "What do you think I'm doing here? I'm here for Nickie."

"She has yoga on Tuesdays."

"*Really?*" I smirked. Like I wasn't perfectly aware of my own sister's schedule. Like I wasn't aware both he and I knew the real reason I was here. "I was hoping to check in, make sure she's doing alright spending 24/7 with you."

McGee didn't take his eyes off me as he slid his arms out of the jacket and placed it on a nearby hook protruding from one wall. Ignoring the open seat next to me, he remained standing. "She's doing fine. Not much to report."

He was making it painfully obvious that I wasn't welcome. But I wouldn't give him the pleasure of watching me leave so soon. Instead, I leaned onto the back legs of my chair, saying, "Are the arrangements still working out? It's funny, you were only supposed to be staying here temporarily. Now you've been here for quite a few years." I gave him a knowing look. "Time flies when you're having fun."

His eyes narrowed and he replied brusquely, "We're doing fine. She likes the company. I run any errands she needs me to and help her out around the house. It works."

"You still visit your parents every month." There was a challenge hidden within the question.

McGee scowled at me. "Yes, actually, I do."

Chuckling under my breath, I moved onto the real reason I made the unexpected visit. "And how is *our* arrangement progressing?"

He stiffened. That was answer enough. "It's going fine. Great, actually. I was just with her now."

"I'm assuming you've given her the Usher already." Silence. "You *have* given it to her by now, right?"

The excuse came quick and practiced. "It wasn't a good time. There were loads of people around, and I thought it would be better if we built our relationship a little more before I—"

My laughter ricocheted around the room, cutting off his last words. The kid reddened. "Well, then. That cash is practically in my pocket already."

"I know what I'm doing," McGee snapped. "I have a plan." I couldn't tell if he was trying to convince me or himself. Either way, it didn't matter. I had my answer.

"Say whatever you want but," I tapped my watch, "time is ticking. Those thirty days will be up before you know it. Then that money will be mine." *And you'll have to admit I was right all along.* Admittance of that fact alone would be enough to remind him of his place.

"I have it under control," he snarled. He gained control of his voice before adding coarsely, "Actually, I need a favor."

I stared at him strangely. This was something I wasn't expecting. "What kind of favor?"

"I need to borrow the car."

"The reason better be good." The chair creaked beneath me as I leaned back and calmly gazed up at him. "You know I don't like when you take it out alone."

"I wouldn't be alone." McGee waved a hand, like he was

trying to brush away his next words. "I'm taking her to prom."

"Wait, wait, wait. Let me get this straight." Sitting forward, I rested my elbows on the sleek wood and put my hands together. "You're taking the same person you're being paid to get hooked to the *school dance*? You're in deeper shit than I thought." I squinted at him as a thought dawned on me. "Don't tell me you're falling for the bitch."

"Don't call—" He stopped. The words he had meant to say hung silently in the air. "It's not like that," he said quickly, but the damage had been done.

For once, I had to struggle to find something to say. I had known the kid for years. During all that time, I had never once witnessed him do something that could put us in jeopardy. Something like this. "I thought you were smart enough to figure this out. You're in deep, kid. There's no option for you to back out now. With those cops sniffing around, I need to be sure you know where you stand. I've told you before, never get attached to the customers." What I said next made him flinch. "I didn't think you were that weak."

He continued to stare at me. Not out of annoyance now, but out of fear. The silence grew exceedingly heavier. My job was complete. Pushing my chair out, I stood and strode to the door. I shoved my arms into my coat and turned to look at him. "I said you were getting too cocky. If you can't handle this gig, you're gonna have to answer to me. Twenty days left." The kid was frozen in place. I put my hand on the doorknob, but paused before turning it. "Say hi to my sister for me."

He still hadn't moved when the door slammed shut.

16 CATHERINE

"Oh. My. Goodness." Eve covered her mouth with one hand, giving me a thumbs up with the other. "Catherine, you look *gorgeous*."

"You think so?" The mirror showed the delicate blue ruffles on the dress which quavered with my every move. "I'm not sure I like this one."

"Why not?" She lightly fluffed the fabric creating an almost tutu-like form around my waist. "It matches your eyes, it's big *and* it's sparkly!"

I ran my hands along the sequins covering the top half of the dress. "I just don't think it's a good fit, you know?"

Eve stepped back to get a better view. "I think I see what you mean," she said thoughtfully. "It needs more . . . poof!"

"No, that's *not* what I mean!" Sliding open the latch on

the dressing room door, I stepped out and glanced questioningly toward my mother. "What do you think?"

She gave me a once-over from her spot on a small bench before replying, "What is Samuel wearing? Maybe that could give us some ideas."

"He's wearing a three-piece. His tie is going to match my dress." I sighed, glancing back toward my reflection. "But I'm pretty sure this isn't what I'm looking for."

My mother addressed Eve, our honorary shopper for the day. She seemed to find hunting through racks of dresses far more enjoyable than my mother or I did. "See if you can find another blue one. Less ruffles, maybe a darker shade of blue."

Eve saluted her military-style. "I'm on it, Claire!" She bustled out of the room, one arm draped with the other rejected gowns. Stepping carefully back into the dressing room, I shut the door behind me and carefully began to slip off the dress.

"Hey, Catherine?" My mother's muffled voice came from the other side of the door.

"Yeah?"

"I haven't had the chance to ask you how it's been going with Samuel."

"Oh. It's been going fine, I guess."

"How long have you been together again?"

I thought before saying, "Almost two weeks, I think."

"That's nice." There was a pause. "Don't get me wrong, I am very happy that you are going to prom with someone that you like. But . . ."

"But what?" I prompted when she trailed off. The dress was a lot harder to put back on the hanger than it had been to take off. My fingers worked the material slowly, hoping that sluggish movements would reduce the wrinkles made in the fabric.

"You've only known him for a few days and he's already taking you to prom. Don't you think it's all happening just a tad fast?"

"It's not like I'm the only freshman going to junior prom. Besides, Samuel was going to go before he met me so he's just adding me to his ticket."

"I know, it's just . . ." My mother's voice was strained. "I can't help but feel like we don't know this person very well."

This person. Did she not even feel comfortable using his name? What was her problem? "It's just a dance. It's not like I'm marrying him."

"Just be careful, okay? Things are moving a little too quickly for my liking. And it doesn't help that he's older than you."

Thrusting open the door just enough to stick my head out, I snapped, "Would you stop it? I get that you're nervous and everything, but Samuel is fine. I know how to take care of myself. We're going to have a great time at prom, so just shut up!"

My mother stared at me with wide-eyes. I'd seen that expression before. My heart dropped when I realized it came onto her face when she and my dad argued. I hated being opposite that look. It was a few seconds before she muttered her soft reply, "Yeah, you're right. I'm over-thinking things." I immediately regretted raising my voice. She didn't need another person yelling at her. But she needed to get off my back. I was old enough to know who to trust.

Luckily, I didn't have the time to form a response. As if she could sense the tension needing to be broken by her contagious smile, Eve reentered the room holding a new gown.

"Mission accomplished!" she exclaimed, excitement lacing her words. "Try this one on! Can you just *imagine* what Samuel will say when he sees you in this?"

17 SAMUEL

"What is Catherine going to say when she sees me in *this*?" I groaned, staring at the monstrosity I'd just been informed was my outfit for prom. My fingers fumbled to button the jacket while I attempted to find an angle that looked decent in the mirror.

"She's going to think that you're the most handsome boy there."

"Shut up, Nickie."

Pulling a hair tie off one thin wrist, Nickie tied her brown hair back into a small ponytail. The dyed-green tips splayed out at the nape of her neck. "You know it's true, Sammy. When you put a little effort out, you tidy up quite nicely."

I ran a finger under the collar, unsure I agreed. The material was too stiff for my liking, too constricting. I pushed back my shoulders and attempted to look professional. "Am I going to be wearing a tie or something?"

"Yes, but we can't buy one until we know what color Catherine's dress is."

"This is all so complicated," I muttered. "I'm regretting the decision to go to this dance more every day."

Nickie elbowed me lightly. "Oh, don't be like that. It'll be nice to step out of whatever you do for my brother, at least for a little while. Plus, you'll get to spend a whole night with Catherine." I remained silent. She didn't know the full extent of Frank's network — or anything about the bet. I hated keeping secrets from her, but it was better that way. If she knew the real reason I asked Catherine to prom . . .

"Oh, c'mon, try to look at least a *little* excited." Placing her hands on my shoulders, Nickie stuck her head around my figure to look in the mirror. "I can't wait to meet her. And you just met her in chemistry class?"

"Yeah."

"So romantic."

"Uh huh."

Nickie scanned my face and rightfully judged that I didn't want to follow this line of conversation any further. "Okay," she laughed, giving my shoulders a final squeeze before letting her hands drop to her sides. "I'll stop being the annoying mom. But don't think I won't expect a full review when you get back." I nodded, then released a sigh of relief when she changed the subject. "So, let's see how our mental checklist for prom is coming along." She began ticking off her fingers. "We've got your suit, so that's a check. You'll need to buy her a corsage—"

"A what?"

"It's a flower bracelet-thing. You'll give it to Catherine when you see her. She'll wear it to show she's not single and she'll pin on your matching boutonniere. You'll also need a limousine—"

I threw my hands up frantically. "No, no way. You're not renting me a damn limo."

"Awh, Sammy . . ."

"No. I already have it planned, I'm taking Frank's car."

"That old POS?" Nickie shrugged when she saw the determination in my face. "Suit yourself." Plucking an invisible particle of dust of my shoulder, she added, "Get it? *Suit?*" I groaned and pushed away her hand. Nickie laughed, then rested one finger delicately on her chin. "Actually, there is one more thing you need to do." Holding out both arms to me, she waved toward me. "Come on, sweetie, let's dance."

"What?" I whipped my head away from the mirror, forgetting my horrific outfit for the first time. "I am not dancing with you, that's just weird."

"Do you actually know how to slow dance?" I threw her

a withering look. "I didn't think so, smartass. Now get over here."

Trudging over to her, I let out a huff of annoyance. "This is ridiculous."

"Oh, give it up. Now, we need a good song . . ." Nickie shot a finger up into the air. "I know just the one." She pulled her smart phone from her pocket, then quickly swiped through songs. I grumbled in protest all the while, but knew it was futile. Once Nickie got something in her head, she wouldn't stop until it had been done. I could tell this was one of those times. A soft electronic thrumming came from the device as she tucked it into her back pocket. She looked up at me and smiled. "Wow, you're taller than I remember."

"I am about two seconds from walking away, Nickie."

"Okay, okay, I get it." Reaching up, she placed her hands delicately on my shoulders. "Now put your hands on my waist." I stared at her. "Don't give me that look. I'm basically your mother, so don't make this weird."

"For some reason that's not making me feel any better," I muttered, but did as she told.

A male's voice joined the music to pick up the melody.

"If this is that song from *Napoleon Dynamite*, I swear—"

"Shut up and start swaying your hips, like this."

I started shifting my weight from foot to foot, looking at Nickie for clarification.

"There ya go, Sammy, you're a natural. Now, at some point during the song, if you feel like it, you can pull her close like this."

I exclaimed in protest when Nickie wrapped her arms around me, placing her head under mine. She was almost the same height as Catherine, right at level to rest my chin on the top of her head. The movement was strictly platonic, I knew that, though I couldn't help but feel out of place.

"Try to enjoy it a bit when you're with Catherine. It's supposed to be romantic."

Listening to the melody of the song, I realized that it wasn't too hard. The rhythm of the tune gave the tempo for when to move my feet. Nickie wasn't a terrible dance partner, either. If I closed my eyes, I could almost imagine I was dancing with Catherine instead.

The final chord was struck and I quickly pulled away. Fully aware of the color in my cheeks, I muttered, "Thanks, Nickie. I mean it."

"No problem." The smile she gave me was sly. "And I have to say, Samuel, you're not a half-bad slow-dancer." I blushed deeper and picked up my street clothes while she laughed. "Now go get changed, you little love-bird."

18 THE BOY, AGE 11

A push from behind sent the boy reeling forward. Landing on the palms of his hands, he grimaced as pain shot up his arms.

"Go home, kid." The boy lifted his head from the pavement. Large, black boots met his eyes. "I don't want no hoodlums in my restaurant." He scrambled up to attempt to explain himself, only to have the door slammed an inch from his nose. Placing a burning palm on the door, he hung his head. That was the problem: he couldn't go home.

A dripping noise started behind him that soon escalated into a steady patter. He turned his face to the sky, letting the rain run into his eyes and mouth. The worn and wrinkled jacket did little to fight the chill beginning to seep under his skin. He shivered, then shuffled down the steps into the back alley of the restaurant.

The boy wandered aimlessly through the streets. As people passed him, they turned their heads away. They didn't make eye-contact. What was it he saw in their eyes: disgust or pity? Either way, it was as if they couldn't see him, a sort of superpower he didn't want. So this is what it felt like to be homeless in the city. When an invisible hand clenched his gut, he remembered why he had tried to steal from the restaurant in the first place. He needed something to eat. That morning, he hadn't eaten breakfast before he left the house. The decision had been spurred by a sudden realization that washed over him during one of his parents' arguments. The fight had been escalating in noise and in consumption of alcohol. He suddenly understood that he couldn't stay in that house a moment longer. In the aftermath of the decision, he wished he'd planned better, or at all. The only item he'd had the foresight to grab was a light jacket, one far too light for the middle of the night in November.

Now, after wandering in and out of shops all day long, it was long past nightfall and he was hungry. Stealing had already been ruled out as an option. The boy looked around and realized he was surrounded by small houses. A sudden idea slipped into his mind which he quickly dismissed. He wasn't that desperate. But once it was apparent he had no other option, he trudged up the stairs of the nearest home. He was given a moment's relief from the rain, courtesy of the small awning hanging above the wooden door. The doorknob was worn and small, thin scratches covering its surface. The boy's heart felt heavy in his chest when he rang the doorbell.

At first, the boy thought no one would answer. He wasn't sure if the thought made him relieved or scared. Right when he was beginning to turn around, the door swung open. A large figure filled the doorway. A slightly overweight woman stared down at the boy in confusion. Her nightgown was plain and frayed around the edges.

"Hey," she said with more volume than was necessary. "What are you doing here? What do you want?"

The boy stared at his soggy shoes. "I was wondering if you had . . ."

She leaned down, cupping one hand around her ear. A lock of long black hair fell in front of her face. "You're gonna have to speak up over the rain. My hearing ain't what it used to be."

"I was wondering if you had any food."

Straightening up, the woman ran a hand over her chin as her expression shifted. "Oh. I see." After a moment's thought, she pointed into the house. "I'll see what I can do."

The boy didn't move when she disappeared into the house. He had frightened himself by what he had just done. Begging was something he never thought he would have to do. But the thought fled from his mind when the woman came back out clutching a water bottle, a small bag of tortilla chips and a slightly bruised apple. "This is all I've got," she said, holding it out. "It's not much."

"Thank you," the boy whispered as he clutched the treasures. His stomach rumbled, mouth already salivating.

"Where do you live, honey?" Silence met her question, and she said, "Do you need me to call anyone for you?"

When he shook his head, the woman kept the door open, looking like she wanted to say something else, before saying goodnight and closing it.

The rain was still coming down in sheets as the boy made his way down the steps. He walked carefully toward a tree planted off to the side of the path. It provided shelter from the worst of the downpour. He put his back to the trunk and slid to the ground, shaking from the cold. A voice to his left made the boy stop, apple poised an inch from his mouth.

"What're you doing here?"

The boy leapt up, fruit still clutched in one hand. A man stood in front of him, tall and slender. Sunglasses concealed his eyes contrary to the fact that there was no sun in sight. He sported a coat that traveled down to his knees, making him seem bulky and taller than he probably was.

Taking a large stride toward the boy, the man repeated, "What're you doing here, kid?"

"Please don't hurt me," the boy blurted, a mixture of tears and rain running down his cheeks. He had heard of what happened to children alone on the streets, and he didn't want anything like that to happen to him.

The man gave a terse laugh. "I'm not going to hurt you." He lowered his glasses to the bridge of his nose, looking over them with squinted eyes. "How old are you?"

"Eleven."

"Where's your family?"

The boy thought and then shook his head. It was easier than explaining.

The man looked at him, then the food scattered around him. Pieces came together in his mind. He suddenly asked, "You like pizza?"

The boy nodded slowly.

"Who am I kidding, what kid doesn't like pizza? How about we go get some pizza and we can talk. How's that sound?" Seeing the boy's expression, the man added, "C'mon, pizza never hurt anyone. We'll just have ourselves a slice and we can chat."

After a moment's thought, the boy nodded again.

"Great." The man gestured him forward, saying, "My name's Frank. What's yours?"

"Samuel."

"Alright, Samuel." Frank led the boy forward through

the open streets. "Let's get you some pizza. I know just the place."

A few minutes later they were seated in the booth of a small Italian restaurant. Frank had a diet soda with lemon and ordered the boy a slice of cheese pizza. He nibbled at it cautiously, glancing around every few seconds. The apple and chip bag was sitting on his lap, like he was afraid someone would steal it when he looked away.

Frank broke the silence. "So, do you want to talk about why you were out on the streets at night in the pouring rain?" The boy glanced away from Frank's eyes. "Come on, kid. I helped you out, you gotta give me some answers. A trade-off."

Shrugging, the boy took another bite. "I didn't go to school this morning."

"And why was that?"

"I left my backpack at home."

"Hm." Frank took a long sip of soda. "Were you in a hurry this morning?"

"I guess so," he replied. Then, quieter, "They were fighting again."

"Who?"

"Mom and Dad."

Creasing his brow, Frank said, "I see. Does that happen a lot?"

The boy's head bobbed up and down. "They're always arguing. They say awful things to each other." Stuffing the last piece of crust into his mouth, he chewed during the quiet. He glanced at the clock, then quickly stood. "It's late. They're going to wonder where I am. I should've been home a long time ago."

"Hey." Frank rummaged in his wallet. Pulling out a twenty, he handed it to the boy. "If you ever leave the house in a rush again, buy yourself some food, alright? I don't want you wandering around again with nothing to eat."

Staring at the twenty with bulging eyes, the boy said, "Thank you."

He turned to leave, but Frank called out after him, "Kid! If you ever need anything else, just let me know."

"Okay," the boy said, and then he was gone.

Frank stayed in the restaurant long after the boy was out of sight, lost in thought.

19 NATHAN

I watched the scrawny teen slink out of the room. His posture was hunched, hands already reaching for the cell phone in his back pocket. As soon as he shut the door, I pulled out my own phone and pressed the familiar contact. "Hey, Therese," I muttered into the mouthpiece.

"Hey, Nate. Not going well?"

"You can tell that from 'Hey, Therese'?"

"It's a skill I have acquired from suffering through long hours with you."

I pushed my shoulder up to hold the phone in place and shut my notebook after a final glance at my notes. "I feel like I'm just going in circles. There's no new information. I played good cop, I played bad cop. I made one kid damn near piss himself from nerves. Either these kids are excellent liars or they're completely clueless."

"Neither of which do I believe is the case," replied Therese with a small laugh. "Remember who we're dealing with here. They're not the brightest bunch, but those who are in on it know their place. There are all kinds of hush-hush agreements among friends and cliques and whatever."

"I know, but I'd hoped we'd at least get something to work with." A mechanical tone came from within a speaker above the door frame. The buzz of conversation began to filter in from the hallway as students were released for the day. "Short of a full-on interrogation, I have no clue how to make them spill."

"Nathan!" Therese's voice chided sharply. "We are not interrogating the students. Most of them are likely uninvolved with this case."

"I never said we would interrogate them. I simply pointed out that it might be a good option."

Therese chuckled, "You never were very patient with teenagers. The best we can do right now is keep working. It's not going to be easy, but we currently have no other choice. I can try another sweep of interviews, coax them into giving us something new."

I rubbed my temple, a headache beginning to press at the sheer idea of the workload. "So we've just got to make do."

Therese heaved a sigh on the other end of the line. "I wish I could give you a better answer, but that's just the way it is. The kids aren't going to snitch unless they're forced to."

There was a brief silence before I conceded, "If they realized how scary this is, they wouldn't hesitate to start talking."

"I don't disagree with you. Until something happens to really frighten them into confession, we're most likely on our own."

My top teeth tugged at my bottom lip thoughtfully. "The way this case is progressing, I'm beginning to prepare for anything."

20 THE BOY, AGE 17

If one glanced at the boy driving the antique Chevy in midday New York traffic, nothing would immediately stand out. He was one of countless others commuting to their date's house before prom night either by car, subway or sidewalk. Each one had a corsage box grasped tightly in one hand and an expectant expression pasted onto their youthful faces. He glanced in his rearview mirror, checking to make sure Nickie was still following him. She had informed him she wouldn't miss prom pictures for the world. Like every other parental figure, Nickie wanted to commemorate the experience as best she could.

But the boy was not like the others. The others weren't half dreading and half looking forward to seeing their date. The others weren't thinking about the time ticking slowly down to the 29th of May.

The others weren't glancing down at the small, rolled joint of laced marijuana sitting in their cup holder.

As the boy attempted in vain to think of anything but the night ahead, he found himself sifting through memories. How had he gotten here: sitting in a borrowed car wearing a three-piece suit, about to go to prom with the girl whose life he was being paid to ruin?

Thinking back, it had started when he first met Frank. His journey had begun there, that night in the pizza parlor after begging at that woman's door. But no, there was never a guarantee they would've ever met again after that. If their paths had never crossed again, nothing else would have come from it. It was the second time Frank and the boy met that changed things.

The boy touched his forehead lightly with one hand, the thought causing a ghost of pain to wash over it. Although the wound had long since healed and the scar faded, the memory still burned bright and painful in his mind.

"You think you're so damn smart, don't you?"

"And what the hell *is that supposed to mean?"*

"You 'say' you can't find a job while I bust my ass working all day—"

"'Say' I can't find a job? I've been searching for—"

"—so you can lay around and watch your damn General Hospital*!" The boy's father slammed the newspaper onto the table,*

thrusting a finger at the open pages. "'Now hiring waitress,' 'open cashier position,' 'looking for nanny'—"

"I applied to all those places!" his mother exclaimed, tears of desperation shining in her bloodshot eyes. "No one called me back. I was thinking, maybe if I went back and finished high school—"

His father barked a crude laugh. "I come home every night to find you drunk off your ass. You don't have enough brain cells left to finish high school."

The boy stood with his back against the kitchen wall, eyes wide. The school bus had dropped him off mere seconds earlier. He hadn't realized what he was walking into. He hadn't even taken off his backpack yet from school. This wasn't the first time an argument greeted him at home, but they had never escalated to this level before. It was as if he were frozen, unable to do anything but watch the heated exchange.

"You know what?" The boy's mother began backing up into the side room. "I'm sick of trying to talk to you. You have no idea what I'm going through."

His father rose to his feet, chair screeching against the tile. "Don't you dare try to walk away from me." She ignored him, striding into the other room. The boy wasn't given a second glance as she passed.

When his father started to follow her, the boy took a step toward him. Maybe if they saw him, they would stop yelling, and ask him how his day was. Instinctively, his father flung out an arm to shove him aside. He was thrown backward. The boy lost his balance, head slamming into the side of a table before hitting the floor. Waves of pain descended on his skull and forced his eyes shut. Lying still, he waited for the hands that would comfort him, hold him, dry his tears.

They never came.

He sat up slowly, the argument continuing through the slight ringing in his ears. Lifting a hand, the boy tentatively placed it to the throbbing pain. His shaking fingers came away stained with blood.

It took a full minute for what had occurred to sink in.

He threw his backpack into a corner, letting it slam to the ground. Grabbing his coat, the boy shoved out the door and took off at a run.

The boy's feet pounded down the street, his breathing short and sporadic. He could barely make sense of which direction he was running through the tears in his eyes. He didn't understand where his feet were taking him until he found himself in a familiar restaurant. The door banged open and other patrons looked up in surprise at the sound. Feeling prying eyes on him, the boy wiped away his tears before stumbling to the nearest open table. Taking deep, gulping breaths, he sat there alone. Only a few minutes had passed before he was interrupted.

"Hey," A voice came from above him. "It's you — ah, Samuel, that's the name."

Raising his head, the boy whispered, "Hi, Frank."

"What are you doing back here?"

The boy pulled a crumpled $20 bill from his pocket. "Buying pizza," he sniffed.

"Wait." Frank leaned down. "Are you bleeding?"

The boy wiped frantically at the wound. "It's none of your

business."

Frank crossed his arms, staring intently at the boy. He took in the blood, the tears, the boy's ratty clothing, his shaking hands. "What happened?"

"It's nothing."

After giving the boy a long look, Frank slid into the opposite seat of the booth. It was clear he wasn't leaving without an answer.

The boy touched the wound lightly again like he was still unsure if it was actually there. "Is it bad?" he asked softly.

"Nah, forehead cuts always look worse than they are. Bleed like crazy."

"Hmm." He murmured, looking at the blood on his hand. "It was . . . an accident. I think."

"You think?"

The boy's expression seemed hopeful, confused and hurt all at once. "I don't know if it was or not. He made me fall."

"Who made you fall?"

His gaze fell to stare at his lap. "My dad."

Comprehension dawned on Frank's face which he quickly concealed. "Did he hurt anyone else?"

"Maybe my mom, but — I don't know." The boy's eyes filled with tears again and he wiped them away angrily. "I don't know why they're doing this. I've seen them fight before, but never like this."

"Do you want me to go back to your house and check on your mom?"

The boy snapped his head up. "No, please don't go there."

"Are you sure? It might make you feel better to know—"

"I don't want you to."

"Okay." Frank raised his hands in surrender. "Well, what're you gonna do now, then?"

Crinkling his forehead at the question, the boy said, "I don't know. Probably walk around for awhile. That's what I usually do."

There was silence before Frank said, "You know, I think I might have something to kill some time. You want to help me out with a bit of work for the day? I'll pay you for it and you can go back to your house when you feel like it."

The boy thought hard. "You'll pay me?"

"Yeah. The work ain't that hard, but I'll give you some cash for it."

The thought of money overwhelmed the boy's apprehension. Cautiously nodding, he stood.

"Excellent. C'mon, kid. Let's get outta here." Frank gripped the boy's small hand in his own and began to lead him toward the door.

Yes, the boy decided as the car crawled slowly down the street. That was when it all began. When Frank gave him his first assignment.

21 FRANK

"You gonna be okay carrying that?"

Giving me a heated glare, Victor shifted the boxes stacked precariously in his arms. "Shut up, you bastard. Just open the door." I smirked at him before shoving into the apartment. The number '7' hanging on the door caught the light and sent a ray of sun into my eyes. Setting my own load down, I gestured to where his should go. He placed it down with a grunt amidst the other labeled boxes.

"I think that's everything."

"Damn right," Victor huffed, swiping the back of his hand across his damp forehead. "These edibles orders are like bricks. They weigh a ton."

Shrugging, I crossed my arms while I caught my own breath. "People seem to love them. Whatever keeps 'em coming back."

Reaching into his pocket, Victor's tobacco-stained fingers drew out a thick cigar. He lit it and took a deep pull. My eyes flicked to the anti-smoking sign pinned crooked to the back wall. We both knew no one would come to enforce it. "Why'd you give this place that stupid name?" Victor asked gruffly.

"Huh?"

"On the phone you called it 'Lucky something.' 'Lucky Seven,' I think it was."

"Oh," I grunted with a laugh. "Old habits die hard, I guess. The kid named this place when he first came here. Has a thing with names, that one. He calls my other apartment Robinson because it's 42. Something about a famous ballplayer." Victor nodded, but I could sense his mind was on other things. He wanted to talk business. "I'm assuming you want to discuss the police and their poking around where they shouldn't."

Victor's eyes narrowed. "I know we were cracking jokes, but this ain't a laughing matter no more." He broke off into a fit of hacking coughs. It took a few seconds for him to regain the ability to speak. "You're the one mixing the stuff those cops are talking about." It wasn't a question. At first I had tried to keep it on the down-low, but it didn't take long for Victor to see the measuring tools and put two and two together.

"Yeah, but I'm not stupid. Customers know what they're getting when they order. Besides, I'm not the only dealer in the city that laces and cultivates their own strains of Mary-Jane. I've got to keep up with competition."

"But out of the whole damn city, the cops have chosen to focus on the blocks you happen to own."

"I've got it covered. Don't worry about it."

He pointed at me with one darkened finger. "That's exactly what I thought you'd say. And is that kid still with you?"

"Who, McGee?"

"Yeah, that one. What's he doing for you?"

"I use him to bring new customers into the system. He's my plant."

"He still staying with Nickie?"

"Yeah. Let's me keep an eye on him."

Giving a grunt, Victor lowered himself to sit on a nearby box. The cardboard strained and groaned under his weight. His dark eyes pierced mine. "You been keeping tabs on where he's going?"

I was growing tired of him asking around the real issue. Small-talk was not something Victor excelled in. "What are you getting at?"

"What I'm trying to say is," he rasped, blowing out a cloud of smoke, "we've got it good, you and I. Money is steady. It's taken us a while to get it this way. I don't need any weak links in the chain threatening that. And I *definitely* don't need some punk kid screwing everything up. 'Cause we both know that once they catch one of us they're gonna start climbing up the system to get to the higher-ups.

"That means if you go down, you're most likely dragging my sorry ass down with you. The main thing they're searching for is where you get your product. Now, I know you well enough to know for sure you won't spill. But that kid . . ." He shook his head darkly. "That kid you took in out of the *kindness of your heart* has a direct tie to you and, therefore, me. If the police were to try and talk him into giving up info about the network, who's stopping him from squealing?"

"I have the kid completely under control. He owes me his life." The sentence tumbled out too quickly. It sounded desperate, like I was trying to convince him. I was careful to slow my next words and gain back control. "He would never dare betray me, not after what I did for him."

"Kids are unpredictable." Victor raised a brow. "I remember what a backstabbing and shifty little runt you were at that age even if you don't. Who's to say McGee ain't the same way? He may be hiding it from you, but he can't hide it from us all."

Much as I tried to come up with something to say, I had no reply. My mind was spinning, thinking of all the opportunities McGee had over the past years to gain intel and inside information about the network. To think that he would betray me was inconceivable after all I had done for him. Or was it? I was paying him to betray people his own age, people that might've once been his friends. Through all that time, I had never stopped to think that he might not be completely honest with me. How could I have been so blind?

I met Victor's stare. There was something that looked like pity behind his eyes. "I hate to break it to you, Frank, but you ain't what you used to be. The years have not been kind to you. You're getting sloppy. To be honest, those two ODs scared the shit outta me. You can't keep your business up with cops breathing down your neck. You gotta think for a second about who you're keeping close to you. Who you're trusting with the important stuff.

"Samuel, the one you keep calling 'kid,' ain't a kid no more. Unless he don't have two brain cells to rub together, he's gonna understand what kind of position he's in and how important he can be to you *and* the cops. What doesn't make it into his head is what could happen if this whole operation blows. If he takes you down, he's takin' all of us down too." Although Victor's voice dropped to barely a whisper, I heard every word. "Watch that kid, Frank. Make sure he remembers who the bad guy is."

22 SAMUEL

Catherine massaged her jaw, slowly opening and closing her mouth. "My face hurts," she complained, frowning at me. "Your aunt was insane about pictures. She must have taken a few hundred."

Smiling in response to her griping, I pressed the gas just hard enough to cross the intersection before the light turned red. "Nickie was just taking advantage of my being in a suit." Upon reflection, the last time I had been in a suit was . . . never, actually. There were never any weddings to go to, religious events, or celebrations. The most I did was put on a collared shirt and tie for picture day at school each year, and even that was enforced by Nickie. If it was up to me, I wouldn't even have done that much.

"I have to admit, you do look pretty spiffy," she replied

with a laugh. "You think she got home okay?"

"I'm sure she's fine. I gave her directions before we left. Besides, if she's really in trouble, she can call me."

Nickie had taken Frank's other car in order to drive back to her place after Catherine and I left. The one I was currently driving was Frank's (and my) favorite. The other was much more mundane, a dark silver truck that could only seat two. Pulling up to Junior prom in that would've turned some heads. To reduce confusion regarding Nickie, I told Catherine that she was my dad's sister. It was easier than explaining our strange living conditions.

Cars blurred as I sped to cruise at a comfortable five miles per hour above the speed limit. I had sworn to myself that I wouldn't make us late to the event we'd been looking forward to for weeks. Well, it was mostly Catherine looking forward to it. Even so, I couldn't deny the butterflies fluttering in my stomach as we continued driving.

We chatted for a few minutes, comparing scores on the most recent chemistry test. Catherine had my number beat by a mere two percent and proudly proclaimed her superiority. At one point, we slowly rolled to a stop and I glanced down the lanes of traffic on either side. "Where am I going?" I asked suddenly.

Catherine glanced at her phone. "The directions say to make a left."

"I think God himself would have trouble finding this place," I muttered, then flipped the steering wheel to make the hairpin turn. "Couldn't they have picked something closer to the school?"

"But where's the adventure in that?"

"Good point."

She cocked her head to one side in thought. "I meant to ask you, why weren't you in class these last couple of days? Chem was boring without you."

"Oh." I swallowed. "I, uh…" Frank had ordered me not to attend school for a couple days until the NYPD had backed off. He didn't care how long it took, as long as there wasn't a risk of my getting caught. Technically speaking, I didn't keep anything on me. At least not while I was in school. Not that I could explain all that to Catherine.

My attempts to throw together an excuse were cut off when a sharp tone echoed through the car. Catherine laughed, looking closer at the cell phone ringing in her hand. "It's my friend, Eve," she explained to my questioning look. "Do you mind if I take it?"

"Not at all. You can even put it on speaker, if you want."

Catherine laughed, "Just so you're aware, I'm not responsible for anything that comes out of her mouth." Pressing accept, she held the phone horizontal toward her face with the speaker toward her mouth. "Hey, Eve."

"Catherine!" Even on the other end of the line, I could hear the smile in the girl's voice. "How are you two doing?"

"We're doing great, heading to the Villa now. You're actually on speaker. Samuel's driving."

I leaned toward the phone while keeping my eyes on the road. "Hello, Eve."

"Hi, Sammy!"

Catherine laughed and looked at me to gauge my response to the nickname. I simply shrugged. It was better than what Frank called me.

"Thank you again for doing my makeup, Eve."

"No problem, girlfriend!" Eve's voice became a whisper, like she was sharing a secret. "Even though you still look gorgeous without it on."

"Agreed!" I shot in and Catherine punched my arm, her face flushing.

"You know, Sammy," Eve added, "I did have money on you for the promposal. All you had to do was make a cheesy sign!"

I suppressed a smile as Catherine chided, "Oh, let it go, Eve! Don't make him feel bad."

"Kidding, kidding!" Eve chuckled, then give a sad sigh. "I'm really going to miss you this weekend, Catherine. Are you sure you can't come down to visit us at the beach house for even a day? You were looking forward to it."

"I told you, I can't. Samuel and I are going out over the weekend."

"I guess that makes sense." It took only seconds for Eve to perk up again. "Well, you two are just the sweetest thing and I know you're going to have a great night."

"Okay, Eve."

"And don't feel bad about not being able to come this weekend. I understand that you two need your *alone time.*"

"Goodbye, Eve."

Catherine pulled the phone away from her face and was preparing to hang up when Eve added, "Also, the second-floor balcony is a great place for a first kiss."

"*Eve!*"

As her friend giggled from the other end, Catherine groaned and clicked the button to end the call. "I am so sorry," she apologized, but even as she spoke her face held a smile. "Eve has no filter."

"It's fine," I chuckled. "It's obvious you two are really close."

"You have no idea." Catherine turned her head to look out the window, moving carefully so as to not disrupt her hair. "We've known each other for way too long. It's impossible to keep a secret around her, she knows me so well."

The Villa came into view a few minutes later, a towering

masterpiece of stone and mortar. Two medieval-style towers rose on either side of a gaping doorway complete with oak doors swinging wide to usher us inside. A wide, red carpet rolled out from within, a tongue on the ground amidst hundreds of brick teeth. Based on what I had read online, the venue was mostly used for wedding receptions and quinceañeras. I hoped they were properly prepared for the chaos our school had to offer. Our last school event, a Halloween celebration, had ended with a group of seniors clad in clown masks terrorizing freshman. That said, the school board had been a bit wary about large student gatherings, but couldn't deny students the long-held tradition of prom.

After stepping out, I strode to the other side of the car and opened Catherine's door. "My lady?"

Smirking at me, she grasped my outstretched hand and stood. Although I had seen her outfit for the first time earlier, I was able to get a closer look at her now that we were side by side and not blinded by camera flashes. Her gown was a midnight blue, standing out from the obnoxious bright pastels that filled the shop windows. It was a waterfall of sheer material, layered to billow with each step. She wore shoes with a slight heel to them, but rather than making her steps seem awkward, they added a grace and maturity to her stride. Wavy hair was placed in a complex array on top of her head, curls cascading down her back.

"What are you looking at?" Catherine asked. She threw up a hand to cover her mouth. "Do I have something in my teeth?"

"No," I laughed, taking the hand covering her face and wrapping it in my own. "You look great. Are you ready to head inside?" Flush receding from her cheeks, Catherine smiled and nodded.

We carefully made our way toward the open doors. Familiar faces waved as we passed and I dipped my head at them in greeting, contrary to the fact I couldn't remember a single one of their names. A newspaper photographer stood off to one side, holding a camera costing more than the car I drove. He took a quick shot of Catherine and me before gesturing us down the red carpet. There were people everywhere, talking and milling about. Flashes dazzled our vision, accompanied by a constant buzz of excited noise.

"Wow," Catherine commented, slipping her arm effortlessly into mine. "This place is kinda overwhelming."

I gave her a pointed look. "So are you in that dress."

Catherine's cheeks turned a darker shade. "Oh, shut up," she jested, and bit her lip before adding, "But I'm glad you like the dress. It took so long to find the right one."

"I don't envy you the art of dress-shopping. I would have no idea where to start with all those colors and styles."

"It was mostly Eve, to be honest. She loves that kind of stuff."

Leading her forward, we pushed past a large group taking selfies. "Let's head inside," I said. "It's getting crowded out here."

The inside was as extraordinary as the outside architecture was, perhaps even more so. A massive chandelier lit by hundreds of decorative candles hung above us, giving the room a warm and bright feel. I noted stained glass windows on our left and right adding additional light to the space. Marble columns pressed floor to ceiling, obviously more for looks than actual purpose. The first open room to our left held a buffet area consisting of every catered food imaginable, complete with an over-the-top chocolate fondue fountain for dessert. Circular tables were set, draped with maroon cloth and vases brimming with flowers placed delicately in their centers.

I turned to Catherine and laughed, "A fondue fountain? They do know that this is a prom, right? And that everyone is wearing super expensive clothes?"

"There is no way I'm risking it," she said, jokingly leading me to give the widest possible berth of the structure. "Not with this gown!"

We paused outside another room, which I assumed was their dance floor. Laser lights flashed indecipherable patterns across the walls while speakers blared hit songs of the year. A few couples and small groups occupied the dance-floor as others slowly filed in through the doors.

"Do you want to dance?" Catherine asked eagerly.

I took a step toward the buffet and gave what I hoped was a convincing smile. "Maybe we should eat first."

"C'mon, there's no one there now. We'll have so much room!"

I weakly replied, "But the food will get cold."

Catching me in my excuse, Catherine stared at me. "You don't like dancing, do you?"

"No!" I exclaimed quickly. "I do, it's just — I, uh, don't have much . . . experience."

"Samuel James McGee." The use of my middle name caused my eyes to roll into my head. She was not fooling around. "I did not get all dressed up to eat cheese and crackers. You need to open up, try something new." She saw my reluctant expression and continued, "Let me rephrase that: Like it or not, you are dancing!" Ignoring my griping, Catherine grabbed my arm and dragged me onto the floor. I'd never seen her be this stubborn about something, but I was slightly impressed at how head-strong she could be when she wanted to. And she was right, the room was pretty empty. The current song was a country hit, acoustic guitar vibrating through the room. A few off-key students accompanied the singer's rich tenor.

Catherine immediately found the beat of the melody and started bobbing her head. She mouthed the words with the ease of much practice. Unsure of where to begin, my foot started tapping out a rhythm. Unimpressed by my lame attempt, she grabbed both my hands and swung them in time with the tune. Students came in a few groups at a time and slowly populated the dance floor. With a few glances toward others, I eventually felt comfortable enough to let go of Catherine. I wasn't the best dancer, but neither was she and no one seemed to care or even notice. It dawned on me that I had never actually danced in public before. There was a nervous thrill to it that sent a rush of adrenaline to my head. And the funny thing was, I didn't hate it.

Within minutes, we could barely move a few inches in any direction. Students pressed in on all sides, moving in time to the music. The dancers eventually parted to reveal a circular spot of floor in the center of the crowd, allowing individuals to step forward. I was content with standing back and watching with Catherine, clapping and cheering.

A few songs in, the music lowered to allow a gruff voice to be heard over the speakers.

"Hey, everyone. This is Jayne, your honorary DJ of the night, speaking. We're going to slow things down a bit for this next song." Couples all around us turned to their partners, nervous or excited smiles lighting up their faces. Those who arrived single or in a group strode out of the room, giggling and whispering to their friends. I watched them leave, nervous energy washing over me. Catherine raised an eyebrow expectantly and, after taking a breath, I carefully wrapped my hands around her slender waist. She placed hers on my shoulders. Her smile seemed to say, *Relax.* My nerves were still strong, but Catherine's confidence radiated out and helped calm them. We weren't doing anything outrageous. It was just a dance.

"For our first slow song of the night, I picked an oldie but a goodie. Hope y'all enjoy."

As the first notes of the song began, I half-laughed and half-groaned.

"Is something wrong?" Catherine asked, staring at me strangely as we began to sway from side to side.

"No, it's just . . ." I chuckled softly before giving a partial lie. "I always think of *Napoleon Dynamite* when I hear this song." There was no way I was telling her about my practice dance with Nickie earlier this week.

Catherine laughed before lapsing into a comfortable quiet. I enjoyed simply staring into her eyes, but after a minute she suddenly asked, "Can I ask you something?"

At first my heart began to race, but it quickly settled. There was no way she could possibly know about my relationship with Frank. So what was there to worry about? As calmly as I could, I replied, "Sure."

"Why me?"

I gave a confused, slightly relieved, smile. "Why you?"

"Yeah." She motioned around the room with her eyes. "There are so many other girls that are far more pretty or smart or popular than me. And I'm only a freshman. So why did you choose me over all of them?"

Her question dragged me out of the blissful ignorance I had lapsed into. The harsh truth rose to my mind, but my voice spoke different words.

Because it was on a bet.

"Because you're not like them."

I'm getting paid to deceive you.

"You're different, and I like that about you."

It was only ever for a bet.

"Don't compare yourself to them."

Catherine drew me close and laid her head on my chest. I breathed in the moment, savoring the feeling of her in my arms. For a few minutes, I decided to forget Frank and the bet and the whole mess. I deserved to enjoy myself. I deserved to know what it felt like to be loved.

With a burst of confidence, I moved my head toward Catherine. Our lips met and the noise and sounds faded away until we were alone. Just the two of us. I allowed myself to melt in her arms, the weight of the stress constantly on my shoulders falling off while in her embrace. The shimmering gloss tasted sweet on her lips and I caught a whiff of her perfume: fresh flowers and vanilla.

For once, I wasn't the Scavenger. I was just Samuel.

When we broke away, breath still caught in my throat, I felt Catherine tense slightly. "Okay," she whispered. "I'm just going to say it. I think I love you."

And contrary to what I was expected to do and what I had been working toward since the very beginning, when I replied, "I love you, too," I realized I truly meant it.

23 NATHAN

I breathed in the fragrant scent of the black tea, letting the steam enter my nostrils and seep down my throat. It sent a current of warmth through my body, thawing my frozen fingers and reaching down to my toes. I held the cardboard cup in the pads of my fingers and prepared to take the first sip of well-earned reward after spending hours out on the open streets.

The door flew open and banged against the wall. My hands carefully grasping the tea jolted at the sudden noise. A few scalding drops fell onto my pant leg, causing me to bite back a curse. "Dammit, Therese," I growled upon recognizing the intruder. "You scared the crap out of me."

"Sorry," Therese panted. She took a moment to compose herself before crossing to my desk. Her chest rose and fell quickly with each breath. "I . . . needed to tell you in person."

Gravity weighed on her tone, alluding to the dark topic she wanted to discuss. I placed my drink down on the desk surface. "What is it?"

My partner paused long enough for me to wonder if she would continue without additional prompting. "Something's happened. Something big."

"With the case?"

"Yes." Therese's hands were twisting once again. Her voice sounded as strained as the motions of her fingers. "I don't think there's a light way to say this, so I'm just going to put it out there."

"Cut to the chase, Therese."

"A student in the high school was discovered unconscious after football practice today." I could tell that wasn't all, so I waited. Her wide eyes remained locked on mine. After a moment, she slowly said, "He OD'd on MDMA laced marijuana, found dead on site."

I blinked, eyes not seeing the office before me. Instead I saw a body, slumped and lifeless as a brother knelt beside it and cried for his sibling to wake up. Parents making funeral arrangements for someone whose birth and death dates were not nearly as far apart as they should have been. Blurred words as a boy attempted to read a eulogy he never dreamed he would have to write.

This was what I had been working against the whole time, to save another family from experiencing the agony I had lived through.

But it was too late. I had failed.

Therese gripped my arm with one hand, leaning toward me. "I know you feel like it's your fault, but it's not. We're doing everything we can—"

"It's not good enough," I said through clenched teeth. My vision was dark around the edges, the emotions roiling inside me barely able to be contained.

"Nathan." Her hold on my arm tightened, her voice pleading. "I can guess what's going through your head right now, but we can't let the past influence this case. If we're going to find out who's behind this, we need keep our minds clear." She attempted to meet my eyes. "I need you with me now. I can't do this without you. Do you understand?"

I nodded curtly. Keeping her eyes fixed on me, Therese drew away with a sigh. She moved with the caution of someone afraid to set off an explosive. It was painfully obvious who that explosive was. When it seemed I had calmed myself, my partner offered, "Now I do believe there is a positive that came from this, though—"

My hand slammed the table's surface, a glimpse of my true fury showing through. "What the *hell* is that supposed to mean?"

Therese put up her hands in defense. "Just listen to what I have to say. We both agree that the kids needed something to scare them into submission, correct?" I remained silent. I didn't trust myself to open my mouth again. "This might be enough to make them talk."

It took a moment for the words to sink it, but the truth of her words slowly became apparent. "I think I see what you mean."

"Now that there's a death toll, things are about to start changing. I was talking to our supervisor this afternoon and it's crucial that we handle this case quickly, but gently. Our superiors wants it capped before it gets out of control."

I stood and grabbed my jacket from the back of my office chair. As I shoved my arms inside and flipped down the collar, I replied coldly, "The thing is, Therese, I'm afraid it already has."

24 CATHERINE

"I can't believe they basically kicked us out," I giggled, hoisting up my dress with one hand and grabbing Samuel's in the other. "What kind of prom ends at eleven? Nobody wanted to leave."

"I believe it," he replied, stepping over to his car while pulling a set of keys from his pocket.

"So." I pointed toward the vehicle. "Is this car yours? Or your parents'?"

"Well . . ." Samuel shrugged. "Kinda. It's borrowed from a friend."

I ran my hand along the sleek exterior. "How old is it? It's in really good condition."

"I think it's a 1990. It's vintage."

"Well, your friend must be super rich. I can count on one hand the number of people I know who own cars in the city." Samuel opened the passenger door, bowing toward me with a majestic hand gesture. I curtsied before stepping inside. My eyes followed his path to the driver's side. "But really, Samuel. Where are we going?"

"I—" Samuel stopped as something caught his eye. I followed his line of gaze, but he was only looking at the cupholder. There were some small objects inside I couldn't quite make out in the muted light.

"What is it?"

He shook his head. "Nothing." Samuel shoved the keys into the ignition. I heard the engine turn over.

"Did your parents give you a curfew?" I asked, attempting to make light conversation.

Samuel gave a crude laugh and pulled out of the parking lot. His remark held a noticeable edge. "My parents don't care what time I get back."

"Okay . . ." I couldn't help but feel I had done something wrong. I tried to bring back the flirtatious, playful Samuel I had witnessed minutes prior. "Did you enjoy tonight?"

Features softening, he murmured, "You have no idea."

The radio station was playing a cheesy love song the girls at our school knew by heart. I made a lame joke about it, but Samuel only gave what looked more like a grimace than a grin and continued driving. There was something off, I could feel it. I didn't know how to address it without sounding like I was prying. Left with no other choice, I sat in the quiet and felt the tension build in the air. This feeling was familiar, I'd felt it before. That night in the city when I mentioned Samuel's parents, and again when I asked why he hadn't been in class. He was cut off by Eve's call, but it felt like he had been preparing an excuse. What would he have said if the phone hadn't rung? Couldn't we trust each other? What was making me feel this way?

He eventually pulled the car off to the side of the road and turned off the engine. I glanced outside, expecting to see some sort of romantic view. Instead, we were parked next to the curb of a dark and dismal street. The shops on either street were closed for the night, leaving almost no light for us to see by. It wasn't a pretty view and something about it made my heart rate pick up.

"Samuel?" I asked slowly. "What're we doing here?" There it was, that sense of dread. It was getting stronger.

His hand was shaking when he reached for something in the cup holder. "I was wondering if you wanted to try something new." Something slender and thin that he held between two fingers caught the light of a streetlamp.

A pit formed in my stomach. "What is that?"

"You don't know what it is?"

"No . . ." But something in me knew I did.

"It's pot. Haven't you ever tried it before?"

"Samuel, what—"

"Just try it." Samuel's voice was strange, pitched different than usual. "It's really relaxing. Pot isn't as bad as some of the other stuff, and this is pure. You'll love it." As he spoke, he pulled a lighter from his pocket. After a few failed attempts, a small flame burst to life at its corner.

"I don't know about this . . ." I'd never seen him act like this before. *What was he doing?*

"C'mon, it's relaxing. Helps take the edge off my nerves." The words seemed forced past his lips. They didn't sound like something he would say. It didn't even sound like his voice. He pressed the tip of the lighter to the joint and held it out to me. "They're even baking it into cookies and stuff now. It's like the newest trend. Most places have legalized it already."

I couldn't take my eyes off the smoking thing in his hand. He was right. I had heard people talking about it. It couldn't be that bad if a lot of people were doing it. My hands were separate from my body as they reached out to take it. A strangely sweet and unfamiliar scent filled the car. It helped Samuel relax and I did feel a little nervous. Wasn't it just the other day Eve was telling me to stop being so uptight? Maybe this could help. Besides, it was legal in a ton of places. That meant it must be pretty safe, right?

But what was I thinking? This was a drug, something I promised myself I would never do. The thing seemed so small, though. So harmless.

"Don't you trust me, Catherine?" Samuel's voice echoed from what seemed like miles away.

I held the thing to my face, every cell in me screaming to put it down. A thin tendril of smoke reached up from one end. The sour scent filled my nose and my stomach lurched. What was I doing? Shame flooded me at the thought of what I was about to do. This wasn't who I wanted to be. I thrust it back at him with shaking hands. "Samuel, *what is wrong with you?*"

25 SAMUEL

When she shoved it back, I couldn't help but sag my shoulders in relief even as my mind reeled. Images rose to my mind of the hundreds of junkies I had dealt with, bags like craters under their eyes, skin drooping off their faces. Because of me, Catherine had almost begun the journey down that path. Marijuana was a gateway to the really dangerous stuff. Who knows how far she would've gone after the Usher?

I tried to remember why I was doing this, why I was trying to ruin this beautiful girl, but nothing I could come up with seemed good enough. Why was I questioning this now, when it was too late to turn back? Why hadn't I thought of this all those years ago?

She jumped when I grabbed the thing from her fingers and tossed it out the open window. "Samuel, what was that?"

The fear in her voice was palpable. She was scared of me. Took her long enough. She should've felt that a long time ago. Looking at her, I could almost imagine the changes that would've occurred had she taken the Usher; eyes slightly glassy, words moving slower past her lips.

Oh God, what am I doing?

I grabbed her shoulders and forced her eyes to lock on mine. "Promise me," I begged, unable to keep my voice from breaking. "Promise me you'll never do it."

"Wait, what?" Catherine started, eyes filling with frustrated tears. "You were just trying to convince me—"

"Shut up," I whispered, shaking her again. The pads of my fingers were white against her bare skin. "Please, just say you'll never do it."

"What the hell is wrong with you?" She pried frantically at my fingers. It was the first time I had heard her curse, but I was too distracted to comment on it. "You're not making any sense!"

"Promise me!"

She froze there, mouth half-open. After a moment, she held hands up in surrender and sniffed, "Okay, I promise."

Vision blurred from the tears in my eyes, I restarted the engine and shoved my foot on the gas. We were thrown back as the vehicle shot forward. My thoughts became incomprehensible as I sped along the city streets.

"Samuel," Catherine asked, voice tight with emotion. "Tell me what's going on."

The words burned in my head, longing to be expressed. Do you know what was in that, Catherine? It wasn't pure like I said it was. It was a special mix of some of the most addictive stuff we have. Frank laced it special for my Scavenger work. If you try it once, it's almost guaranteed you're hooked. Do you know what could've happened if you had listened to me? What damage would've been done?

"No, I won't accept that." I'd never heard her this upset. Emotion strained her vocal chords, words breaking as they passed her lips. "There's something going on with you and I'm not taking silence as an answer. Tell me what's wrong."

"I can't," I whispered.

"Please try."

I shook my head, eyes burning with unshed tears. "Not now."

"Samuel." She was begging now. "At least tell me where we're going."

"Where I should have taken you the moment we left prom."

Houses lined every street we passed, lights turned off for the night. I barely registered where I was driving, mind working on frantic autopilot. Less than a minute later, I pulled to a stop in front of her house. It crossed my mind that someone might smell the pot on her, but I was too drained to think of a reason if it was questioned. Deep down, I hoped they would catch me and make me pay for what I had tried to do.

Catherine stepped out of the car. Her hair was frizzy and disheveled now, light mascara tracks running down her cheeks. Even the dress was worn and wrinkled. Through the open door, she pleaded, "Talk to me."

I reached over the seat to grab the door handle. She jumped when it slammed shut in front of her. Gripping the steering wheel so tightly I felt my knuckles pop, I drove away.

26 NATHAN

"State your name."

"William Elliot."

"Grade."

"Junior."

I glanced toward Therese, verifying she had finished jotting everything before continuing. "What can you tell us about the drug network rumored to be infiltrating your school?"

William squirmed in his chair, refusing to make eye contact. He was a well-built kid, muscular arms courtesy of years playing varsity sports. The jacket covering his shoulders had 'Basketball' emblazoned on its back in bright yellow against as dark blue. Contrary to his athletic background and my prior experience with high school jocks, the posture he held was the opposite of confident.

"Well," he began. "I dunno much."

"Whatever you can tell us would be extremely helpful," Therese replied lightly.

"Mmhm." William seemed to think carefully before continuing. When he did speak, he swallowed his words and I had to strain my ears to catch them. "I know there's a lot of people involved."

"Okay," I said tersely. This was wasting my time. "Can you tell us anything specific about those people?"

"I mean, I've seen people doing pot and stuff, but I dunno any of their names." Therese and I shared a look, minds working together.

Clasping my hands together in front of me, I placed my elbows on my knees and leaned forward to meet his eyes. He shifted to move away from me. On edge, nervous. "Can I call you Will?" He nodded, apprehension apparent. "Why are you here, Will?"

"Huh?" His voice was confused, but his eyes betrayed utter terror.

"We were just about to wrap up here when you walked in," Therese explained, picking up on where I was headed. "You asked us for an exception to meet with you."

"I . . . uh," the kid stammered, "I wanted to help, y'know?"

"I'm going to be quite frank with you, Will." I gave him

a small smile. "I've been sitting in this damn chair all day listening to nothing but useless info I already know. I think you may be able to help us." Whether that was true or not, I still needed to decide. "You don't have to worry about any repercussions; we know you're not the problem. We're after bigger fish, and I know you can help us find them."

William sat there silently, growing increasingly agitated by the second.

Therese clicked her pen shut. "We won't be able to help you unless you're honest with us."

William opened his mouth, closed it, opened it again. "I really don't know much," he said, "but I do want to help. I don't want anyone else to get hurt."

I prompted, "Let us decide if what you know is 'not much.'"

"Okay." He relaxed his shoulders and began, "I've started noticing things. I ain't that smart and all, but I do notice patterns. Like in basketball. You watch the way the defenders move, see how far they can stretch, how fast they dribble—"

"Patterns, yes, I understand," I interrupted, eager to get to what was important. "What did you notice?"

"There's been this black car that sometimes parks outside the school and drives around. It's been doing it a lot recently, which is why I noticed it."

Now we were getting somewhere. "Could you tell what type of car it was?"

"I ain't a mechanic or whatever, but I think it was pretty old. Smooth and black, New York license plate. Definitely some sorta sports car. Wasn't able to pick up the number, though."

It wasn't one of our guys. Even if someone had been assigned, they wouldn't have parked outside the front of the school. "What makes you think they're involved in the investigation?"

"Well, I noticed there's this one guy that always drives the car." William was talking more freely now that he had begun. "I'm pretty sure he's a guy, but all the windows are tinted so it's hard to make out age or anything. There was one time I got real close to the car and I swear I smelled pot." Realizing what his words implied, he shook his head quickly. "Not that I'm around weed often, but I know what it smells like, being in such a big school and all—"

"It's quite understandable, William." Therese's voice was calming and cajoling. "We don't think you're behind this. Just keep going."

"Alright. But it just seemed outta place, y'know? So if there was something going on, I think it's with that old car." It was a second before he added, "That's all I got."

"That was very helpful, William," Therese said, making a

final note in her journal. "Thank you."

"No problem." William sat for a second in silence, then stood and hustled toward the door. He seemed to want as much distance between us as possible.

"That was something new," Therese commented, looking over her notes. "We might actually be getting somewhere. I don't think he was actually involved, just a nervous wreck with a good heart. It's a shame he didn't give us a connection to anything specific."

"Doesn't matter," I replied. "He gave us something to start with." Leaning back in my chair, I said thoughtfully, "You know, Therese, I don't want to get my hopes up, but that car could be the first step in solving this case."

"You think so?" My partner scanned her notes, looking thoughtful. "I wonder if any of the other students know anything else about it. All this time we were focusing on drugs and should've been looking into cars. I'll start asking about it during the second round of interviews."

It wasn't much to work on, it but it was more than we started with. And it might've just been enough to catch the bastard behind this.

27 CATHERINE

"Hey, it's Samuel. I—"

"Damn!" Stepping to the side of the busy sidewalk, I impatiently waited for his voicemail to finish.

Beep. "Samuel, pick up the phone. I don't know what happened last night. I just want to talk. Please call me back." I swallowed and tried to think of something to say. "Samuel . . . I don't know what to do." After hanging up, I massaged my temple with one hand while attempting to gather my thoughts. Last night had ended in a blur, with his car speeding off in a scream of tires and the scent of burnt rubber. Nothing had made sense and I went to bed in an exhausted haze. Once my eyes opened that morning, I immediately called Samuel. When he never picked up, I dialed again. And again. He never responded. By lunchtime I was sick of being cooped up in the house, waiting for an answer I wasn't sure I'd get. I began walking the streets of New York, glancing at my phone every few seconds to make sure I hadn't missed a notification. At least being out on the streets made me feel like I was taking steps forward. What direction I was actually taking them in, that was another story.

Shutting my eyes, I tried to think of a plan. Finding Samuel was the only way I would get answers. Brainstorming places he could be led to countless dead-ends, seeing as I had never even been to his house. He didn't even have a 'home phone' I could call. I had nothing to go off of except a useless set of ten numbers I had dialed more times than I could count. It was almost like he didn't want to be found.

I was seriously contemplating turning back when I felt the phone buzz in my hand. Shoving it up to my face, I read the alert.

Samuel: I'm in Central Park.

It was all I needed. Stumbling around the people in my path, I started running. In the minutes it took to arrive, my mind whirred with what could've caused him to do what he did. But nothing I came up with seemed to make any sense. The only way I would figure out any of this was to talk to him face to face.

I skidded to a stop on the outskirts of the park. The

wind had picked up, blowing frail blossoms off the full trees and sending them flying. Crossing my arms against the chill, I scanned the area. My eyes fell upon a figure sitting alone near the pond. He was hunched over, collar turned up against the breeze. Carefully stepping towards him, I felt the ground give a little underfoot. He remained motionless when I sat down beside him.

"Hey, Catherine," he said.

"Hey, Samuel." I tried to look at his face, but it was turned away. Silence grew like a physical barrier between us.

"I just want to say . . ." He trailed off, then turned to me. His eyes were glassy, skin pale. If I didn't know better, I would've thought he was ill. "I don't know what I want to say. I have no clue what came over me." We locked eyes before Samuel's gaze darted away. He couldn't look me in the eye. What happened in the car after prom wasn't by chance or sudden change of heart. I knew for certain now: he was hiding something.

"I just want to know why." I said, keeping my voice even. "You were acting weird last night, but I think it goes deeper than that. I know you've been keeping things from me, and I think it's time I heard the whole story."

Samuel turned to me, eyes shining. "Story?" The way he said the question held the answer.

"I feel like there's a part of you I don't know." I put into words the question that had been settled in the back of my head for a long time. There were two people missing when we took prom pictures, two people I had never seen even after all this time. "Samuel, what happened to your parents?"

It was as if a physical weight pressed upon his shoulders, forcing them down. He curled in on himself. Feeling like I had to do something to ease this pain, I placed a tender hand on his shoulder. A tear rolled down his face, leaving a damp track in its wake. "You want to hear . . . everything?" he asked, and I nodded. He took a rattling breath before beginning.

28 SAMUEL

How much could I tell her? What was too much or just enough? I needed to think fast. I didn't have time to think things through.

"Everything started off great. We were like every other family living in the city. I was happy with just the three of us, never wished for a sibling or anything. My mom used to take us up to picnics at Weehawken and we'd spend family time together. We got along fine. I mean, they fought like couples sometimes do, but nothing too bad."

That wasn't giving away too much information. I had to decide how much to tell. I knew what Frank would do if I told her too much. There was no question in my mind that he would kill me. Not only that, he would go after Catherine, too. I couldn't put her in that kind of danger. But I had to tell her something.

"As I got older, the arguments became more frequent. Then, they started drinking more. I don't know what made them crack, but one day I came home to find my mom laying on the couch when she was supposed to be at work. She had been drinking. After that, something flipped, like a lightswitch. They started acting differently, towards me, towards each other. It only got worse from there; both the drinking and the fighting. Months went by. I prayed for it to go back to the way it used to be, but it never did. Sometimes it would get so bad, I would just run away from it all. Ditch it, get lost in the noise of the city."

I was still telling her the truth. We were getting to the crucial moment. Could she tell if I was lying?

"One day, I stayed out all day and into the night. I was so hungry and looking for food."

My mind waited with bated breath to see what my mouth would say.

"I met this guy and . . ."

He introduced me to the drug market.

". . . and he . . ."

"He what?" Catherine prompted.

"He . . ."

This was it: *choose.*

"He gave me my first joint. Got me hooked. I've gotten better with time, but the craving never really goes away."

It was a lie. Over all the years I'd been a part of this, I'd never actually used the drugs. I just dealt them. But I needed to give her a reason, any reason. She would've hated me if she knew the truth; though not as much as I despised myself.

"Last night I got so flustered. I didn't know what I was doing."

I couldn't do it. I couldn't tell her everything. I may have just saved my life, but it was only a matter of time before I ruined hers.

"I'm so sorry," I whispered, the words having a double meaning I knew she wouldn't understand.

She mulled over the words, seeing my story add up. A few seconds passed before she said, "It's okay, Samuel." I felt her arms grasp me and I almost pulled away. *No, I don't deserve your love. I don't deserve your affection.* "We can get through this. But we can't keep anymore secrets from each other."

She didn't understand the tears pooling in my eyes. The secrets I kept were becoming unbearable to hold. How far would I go to make sure Catherine stayed in the dark? What would happen when I couldn't keep silent any longer?

29 NATHAN

"That about wraps it up, I think," Therese said. She locked the office door and moved to stand behind where I was currently seated. Placing a hand on my shoulder, I felt her lean forward to look at my computer screen. The monitor lit up in front of me was currently at maximum zoom. I ignored her and squinted at the blurry numbers before muttering another curse. The plate was indecipherable. With a tentative glance toward me, my partner asked, "I take it it's not going well?"

"No shit." I shot back. My eyes were aching from hours of concentration. I attempted to massage them while saying, "That son of a bitch knew the exact distance to park from the school so the cameras couldn't pick up the plates. There's no way I'm getting a read on any of these numbers. With chances of him coming back to the school getting lower by the day, I have no clue how we're going to find him. Uh, what are you doing?"

For the last few sentences of my assessment, Therese had covered her mouth with one hand and had been nodding with exaggerated concern. "Oh, nothing," she bubbled. "Are you done?"

I squinted at her. "Yeah."

My partner removed her hand from her mouth. She had been concealing a smile. "Are you ready for my conclusions?"

"Your what?" I could barely think straight, mind hazy from the monotonous work.

"My conclusions from the second round of interviews."

"I need a drink," I muttered. "Yeah, go for it."

"Are you sure? I just want to make sure you're fully finished—"

"I swear to God, Therese, just spit it out and wipe that damn smirk off your face."

My partner cleared her throat loudly before explaining, "Well, the round of new interview questions went smoothly. Most just gave lukewarm answers as to whether or not they have seen the car." She gave a shrug. "Besides that, I only found out that one of the students was seen getting into the car."

There were exactly two and a half seconds of silence before I violently swung the chair around to gape at her. "*One of the students got into the car?"*

"Yep. I had two people mention it. Check the camera recordings for—"

"That's what I'm doing," I confirmed, already typing frantically at the keyboard. "Do you have a date?"

"One of them mentioned about two weeks ago. Both sightings occurred after last bell," Therese reported, leaning over my shoulder to stare intently at the screen. Swiping through the array of camera footage, I found an angle where I could just make out the car in the back. I sped through the first few minutes and pressed play just as the students began filing out through the school doors. It took a couple attempts before I found what we were looking for.

"There it is," I muttered, touching the pad of my finger to the pixilated car. "And here they come."

"Look." Therese pointed to a sweatshirt concealed boy. He had been walking alone, but suddenly turned to stride quickly toward the car. "That's him. That's Samuel."

"We have a name?" My eyes stayed fixed on the kid as he got into the passenger seat.

"Samuel McGee. He's a junior. I was able to confirm it between the students who had seen the car. I was preparing to call him in for an interview, but he hasn't been in school for the past couple days. His attendance is sporadic at best. Samuel comes in just enough to evade loss of credit. His house phone isn't answering. I've asked the principal to send the parents an email, but there's been no response on that front either." Therese nodded toward the car on the video. "If there's anyone who I would say is trying to avoid getting caught, it's him."

"Samuel McGee," I breathed, watching as the car drove away from the school. "What are you hiding?"

30 FRANK

The dial tone rang in my ear and I smashed the phone onto the table. I heard the screen crack and felt the sting of glass shards in my hand, but was too blinded by fury to care. Of all the times for an overdose to happen, why *now?* The cops would be even more on my case now. I'd have to hunker down with regulations, make sure I knew where everyone was at all times. I was so lost in thought I almost didn't hear the door slam and footsteps running up the stairs. By the time I spun around to face the intruder, McGee was already pushing open the door. As he stepped inside, I turned to face him while rapidly shifting my demeanor to hide my rage.

"Where were you last night?" I asked briskly, watching him carefully. "You didn't come back after prom."

His eyes flicked around the room. When he spoke, the

words tumbled out of his mouth too quickly to be natural. The speech had been prepared beforehand. "We drove around for a couple hours. I was running low on gas and I would've refilled the tank, but didn't have any cash on me. I ended up sleeping in the car after I dropped her off." He gestured to my shattered phone on the desk. "I left a voicemail about it." Seeing I wasn't about to give a reply, he shoved back his shoulders and stated, "Frank, I have something to tell you."

"Go ahead."

Shutting his eyes, he blurted, "I don't want to be a Scavenger anymore."

I stared at him.

"I can't be involved in any of this. It's too much pressure. I was thinking about moving out of the city, getting a real job." I advanced toward him. His voice grew quieter and less assertive with each step. "I'm leaving tonight. I'll give you the five hundred for the bet. I swear on my life I won't tell anyone about you, or the bet, or—"

"*Forget about the bet!*" Striding quickly, I grabbed him roughly by the hair and slammed him against the back wall. The kid let out a cry, straining in my grip. After listening to his frantic breaths, my mind finally caught up with my actions. I unwound my fingers from his hair and stepped back. He stayed against the wall, frozen in place and pale as stone.

"Do you remember Daniel Tamivore, Samuel?" I asked suddenly. There was a pause. McGee nodded cautiously, unsure of where this was headed. The rest of his body was a statue, pale and unmoving. "You were assigned to bring him into the network, what was it, two months ago?"

"I did," McGee said. His gaze flicked toward the open door. I quickly moved to stand between him and it. He wasn't going anywhere.

Pointing to my desk, I continued, "I just received a call that he overdosed on a mix of Molly and MJ. Died a few hours ago." Although it seemed impossible, McGee grew paler. That was one of our mixes and he knew it. "The police are conducting full interviews at the school, Samuel, and do you know what that means?" I took a step toward him. "That means when they ask those kids who Daniel spent time with before he died, fingers are going to point to you." I advanced toward him and my voice rose in volume. "It is too late for you to 'get out' now, Samuel. You are in this, now and forever." The kid was at a loss. Whatever he had been expecting, it wasn't this. But I wasn't finished yet.

"A few days ago, I was informed of some concerns that you are not fully committed to this cause. That you may be attempting to back out or even turn towards the police for assistance."

Samuel visibly started. "I would never—"

"Now, that's just crazy, Samuel, because you know that if you ever attempted to double-cross me, they will find you in a ditch." The mirthless laugh I gave made him shudder. "So you see, unless you were completely brain dead, there would be no reason for you to leave my side."

McGee's face was completely blank save his eyes, which darted around, searching for an escape. He tensed when I placed a hand on his shoulder. It rose and fell with his shallow breaths. "Here's what I'm going to do, Samuel. I'm going to pretend that I never heard what you said when you walked in here. In exchange, forget about going back to that high school until the police back out. You're assigned street-work until you regain my trust. Does that sound like a fair deal?"

His eyes were wide, staring straight ahead. They betrayed his fear. "Yes."

I wrapped an arm around his shoulders. "I knew my Scavenger wouldn't let me down."

31 SAMUEL

The door locked behind me with a click. Leaning my weight against it, I allowed myself to slide to the floor. My head fell to rest on my knees and I released the tears I had been struggling to hold back. I killed Daniel. He had been taking that stuff because of me. If I had never shown it to him, he would still be alive. And Frank was asking me to do the same to Catherine. How could I live with myself?

"You're home early."

I quickly dried my face, knowing full well she had already seen the tear-tracks. "Hi, Nickie."

"What is it, nine?" she said with a casual glance toward her watch. "I'm not sure I've ever seen you come home two hours before curfew." She was clad in a hot pink bathrobe, hair squeezed into curlers pressed tight against her head.

"I'm just really tired." I stood and gave my shirt a half-hearted tug downward in an attempt to straighten my appearance. "If you don't mind, I'm going to head to bed."

As I attempted to walk past her, she caught my arm. "Is there something you want to talk to me about?" Her face asked questions I wasn't sure I could provide answers to.

I turned toward her. There were so many things I wished I could say, but none that I could put into words. "I think . . . I need some advice."

"I thought so." Nickie motioned downwards. "Let's sit." I smiled sadly at the familiar action as we both lowered ourselves to sit on the tile floor. Nickie was never one to care much for furniture. She had always preferred sitting cross-legged on the ground than being confined to a chair. Years ago, I used to do all of my homework on the ground with her, papers spread around us in a semi-circle. It was calming, therapeutic almost, to relive those comforting moments. "What's up?"

I traced my finger in the ridges of grout mindlessly. "Have you . . . did you ever . . ." I struggled to put my thoughts into coherent words.

Turned out that I didn't need to; Nickie understood even with my fragmented thoughts. When her eyes narrowed slightly and she gave me her signature look, the look that meant she could practically read my mind, I knew she was putting the pieces together. Sitting back on her hands, she said, "You know, Samuel, I'm not stupid. I'm aware of what my brother dragged you into, so you don't have to hide it from me." I hung my head, staring at the rough stone. "I never wanted you involved from the beginning. He reassured me it would never get to be too much for you." She reached forward to lovingly cup the side of my face in one hand. I didn't realize until that moment how much I missed motherly affection. "Now look at you. I can see the weight of what you're carrying in your eyes. It's not secrets that are dangerous, Samuel. It's what secrets make people do."

The tears were falling again, traveling down my face and under my chin. Nickie used one thumb to wiped them away, saying, "I know from personal experience how cruel my brother can be. But you have to stand up to him. I have no idea what he's having you do this time. Whatever it is, it's changing you and not for the better. If you truly feel that Frank is making you do something you can't follow through with, then you need to trust that instinct." She tilted my head up toward hers. "Just remember that Frank is going to take your departure very seriously. Please be careful. My brother can react very strongly to those who defy him."

Nickie wrapped her arms around me and I gripped her back. Words were exchanged silently between us and I knew she understood. She was aware of the decision I had to make.

"I can't help you make this choice," she whispered, "but

whatever you decide, I will stand behind you." I squeezed her tightly in gratitude. We broke apart and rose to our feet.

I drew a hand across my eyes, wiping away the last of the moisture. There was no time left for tears. There were things that had to be done. "Goodnight, Nickie."

As I walked toward my bedroom, I heard her soft reply: "Sweet dreams, Sammy."

32 CATHERINE

Pushing aside the curtain, I confirmed that the street outside my house was still empty. 5:50 blinked obnoxiously on the watch encircling my wrist. Eve had informed me she would arrive home around six, but she always exaggerated her ETA so she could get places early. That would put her to arrive at my house right about—

A rumble accompanied the silver car that turned down my street. Even through my bedroom window I could hear the music blaring from within the vehicle. It screeched to a halt at the foot of my driveway and the back door opened. Eve stepped out, hauling a neon green suitcase behind her. She waved to the driver before starting up my driveway. Her attire included flip flops, brightly colored leggings and an oversized t-shirt. The doorbell rang just as I reached the foot of the staircase.

"Catherine!" Eve exclaimed when I opened the door, dropping her suitcase to wrap her arms around me. She smelled vaguely of sunscreen and fast food. "How was your weekend?"

"It was fine." Hoping she would leave it at that, but knowing she wouldn't, I led her inside and prompted, "I want to hear all about the beach-house."

"Oh." She brushed aside a piece of hair from in front of her face. Now that we were closer, I could see her cheeks held a constant blush courtesy of a light sunburn. "It was pretty small, but there weren't many of us so size wasn't a problem. The beach was gorgeous! We swam all day and went to a bar at night. Don't worry, no drinking or anything — just frozen lemonade and stuff."

"You're the last person I'd expect to underage drink, Eve," I laughed, pushing her bag into an empty corner and walking into the kitchen. Walking to the fridge, I opened it and asked, "On that train of thought, do you want something to drink?"

"Nah, I'm good." Remembering suddenly, she exclaimed, "Hey! You spent the whole weekend with Samuel. *Alone.*"

"Yeah," I confirmed. The glass of iced tea was gripped tightly in one hand, my other clenched at my side. *Please take the hint, Eve. It wasn't what I thought it would be.*

"Elaborate! C'mon, what'd you do for three days? You two looked adorable at prom. We were all talking about it at the beach house."

I sat across from her and took a long sip before answering. I'd say just enough to pacify her. "Well, after prom we just sort of talked and drove around for awhile. We went for a walk in Central Park on Saturday, but nothing huge. It was nice to just hang out without any pressure."

Although nothing I said was an outright lie, she must have heard something beneath my words because she moved her seat closer to mine. "Is that really it?" she said. Her question was slightly accusatory, which made me straighten. "I was hoping for something a little more — detailed."

"That's it. I told you, Samuel's not an over-the-top kind of guy."

Eve sighed. "It's a shame you didn't come with us. I think you would've liked the beach."

"Samuel asked if we could just stay home. He said he wanted some quiet one-on-one time."

"That's understandable." She paused, staring at me peculiarly, before adding, "Are you sure that's all? I don't mean to press, but I can't imagine you did nothing even the least bit interesting all weekend. Besides — you seem a little off."

"I'm fine."

The response was too quick to be sincere. Eve narrowed her eyes slightly at me.

"The thing is, Catherine," she said slowly, "I don't think you are." Gathering her breath, she met my eyes defiantly. "To be blatantly honest, I'm not sure Samuel is good for you."

"What? Eve—"

"Please, just hear me out." I could tell she'd had this on her mind for awhile. "He seems nice enough, but I'm getting a different type of intuition about him now. The way you talked about him, just now ... it sounded like you were scared." I couldn't meet her eyes. "When we first met him, we knew nothing about him. Come to think of it, we still don't know much. I heard you yelling at your mom when we were dress shopping, Catherine." That made me look up and start to protest, but she interrupted, "I don't want to get involved in your personal matters, but what she brought up was a valid point. This boy was, and is, still a stranger. I mean, you haven't even been to his house. And you're changing. We used to be so close, but I feel like you're keeping things from me."

Eve was really concerned. Ever since we were young, I would share everything with her. We knew each other's biggest secrets. Didn't she deserve to know this one?

"To be honest . . ." I couldn't keep my thoughts hidden

any longer. I needed to tell someone. "I have been getting some — weird vibes from him."

"Okay," Eve said, relieved at my honesty. "What do you mean, weird?"

"It's kind of hard to explain. He just seems — different." I rolled the cup in my hands, not meeting her eyes. There was no way she could understand. I shouldn't have even tried. "You know what, forget I mentioned it. I'm sure he's fine."

"Are you sure? The way you're describing it doesn't sound fine."

"No. Just drop it."

"But Catherine—"

"I said drop it, Eve!"

My friend jumped a little. I could feel her eyes on me when I took another sip of iced tea. It seemed more bitter than when I had first poured it. "Well," Eve said slowly, "I guess you really don't want to talk about it." That sentence held another question, but I refused to rise to the bait. There was an uncomfortable silence. Eve waited a moment before sighing. "But if you ever need to talk, I'm there for you. You know that, right?"

I responded with a curt, "I know." After a few seconds silence, Eve expertly switched topics and began talking about dress styles from Friday night. It was an attempt to lighten the atmosphere, but I couldn't participate. Somehow, a conversation that would've once intrigued and excited me now seemed bland and mundane.

The anger I felt shouldn't have been directed at her, I knew that. Eve only wanted to help. Something in the back of my head whispered that the situation with Samuel wasn't resolved, that it might be getting worse, but I ignored it. I could handle myself. Nothing that Samuel hid couldn't be worked out together.

33 SAMUEL

I can't believe I'm doing this. The thought ran circles round my head as I drove. I was leaving New York, permanently. This wasn't something I could do spur of the moment. Frank and the rest of the networking mess would stay behind while I moved far away. I had left a note for Frank in an attempt to explain. I couldn't face him in person, especially since I was using his car to get away. I would trade it in as soon as possible and pay him back when I could. It was a shaky plan at best, but all I knew was that I couldn't stay in the city a moment longer. Hopefully he would understand. I had already talked to Nickie about it. The image of her fighting back tears when I pulled the car into the street was burned into my mind.

That left one loose end.

I had been putting off calling Catherine the most because

it would mean I would have to reveal everything I had been hiding. There was no knowing how she would react when I told her about Frank, or the network; or the Scavenger. Part of me wished I could break the news in person. Another part of me was glad we had the space of telephone signals between us.

Scanning the view outside to make sure there were no cops nearby, I pulled out my cell phone with one hand and kept the other firmly on the wheel. Getting pulled over now would burn up valuable time. After hesitating, I forced myself to press call. I had no choice. It was time.

Catherine picked up after two rings. "Hello?"

"Hi, Catherine."

"Oh. Hi, Samuel." Her voice seemed off. It was almost like she knew something was wrong. Whatever she thought she knew, it was nothing compared to what I was about to tell her.

"I need to talk to you. Are you alone?"

"Yeah." I heard the muffled noise of a television on the other end of the line. "I'm at home. Where are you? What's going on?"

My heart felt leaden in my chest. "I have something to confess."

"Okay." She sounded only slightly caught off guard.

A horn went off in the car beside me and I had to wait

for the noise to clear before continuing. "I . . . I'm not who you think I am."

"Was that a car horn? Are you driving?" There was a lengthy pause. "Wait, what?"

"I've been lying to you. A hell of a lot more than I should have." The truck a few hundred feet behind me reminded me of something, but I couldn't quite place it. I lost the train of thought when I heard Catherine's hushed words.

"About what?"

Where to start? "Well, I don't live with my parents."

"Oh," she said slowly. "Then who do you live with?"

"It's a bit confusing, but I stay with . . ." The man sitting at the wheel of the truck I was looking at came into view. The sight instantly sent a jolt of recognition through me. "Frank," I breathed. The realization suddenly crashed over me. He had two vehicles, not just the one I was driving. The second was behind me, maintaining an uncomfortably close distance. He knew. He knew everything.

And he was coming for me.

"Frank? Who's Frank?"

"No," I said distractedly, glancing from the road to the mirror. "I don't live with Frank, I live with his sister. But that's not important." He was gripping the steering wheel with white knuckles. Even in the reflection, I could see his eyes flash with fury. My eyes were glued to the figure in the mirror as he reached inside the inner folds of his jacket. "Listen, Catherine, I have to go. I'll call you back." Could she hear the panic in my voice?

"Wait, what? Samuel, what're you doing? Where are you?"

"I'm on the road, but—" The afternoon light caught on the object in his hand and I nearly dropped my phone. "Oh, God. He has a gun."

"Did you say *a gun?* Samuel—"

I ended the call and dialed Frank's number. Maybe if I could talk to him, make him understand ... but no. It went to voicemail after ringing for what seemed like eternity. If the phone was with him, he didn't pick it up. I threw the phone into the back seat and carefully placed my hands back on the wheel, breathing hard. My brain kicked into overdrive, desperate to think of a plan. I couldn't talk to him when he was in a state like this. Nickie had warned me he had a tendency to react first and ask questions later. Over the years, I'd witnessed his outbursts first-hand. With that gun in the passenger seat, I couldn't give him the opportunity to use it. If there was a way I could lose him, on the highway or on a side road, that might give me the chance I needed to get away.

I deftly turned the wheel toward the nearest exit, my heart sinking when Frank did the same. He wasn't trying to hide. He wanted me to know he was coming.

The road became vacant apart from our two vehicles. It was an empty street, sporadic stores lining its sides. I was aware that if I kept driving for only a few more miles, I might be able to get away once I reached the highway. Thinking it was worth a try, I pressed the gas a little harder. Frank picked up speed to keep the distance. If I could somehow cut him off—

A soft beeping came from the dashboard. There was a light blinking that I hadn't noticed before. "No no no no," I breathed. "There's no way I'm out of gas, not now." Staring at the symbol, I waited for it to disappear. This simply couldn't be happening. I remembered telling Frank I didn't have money for gas. Of all the times to forget to refill the tank . . .

The car was slowing down. I pushed on the gas and the car gained a small burst of speed, only to lose it a second later. "C'mon!" I screamed, slamming a hand down on the steering wheel. "No, please . . ."

I kept the gas pedal on the floor as the car rolled to a stop. Frank's truck pulled behind me. I watched with bated breath as he opened the door. The area surrounding us gave me a glimmer of hope. We were in a small development. There was a person walking their dog across the street. He wouldn't kill me out in the open. Maybe I had a chance at getting out of this alive.

Frank walked between his vehicle and mine, hands clenched at his sides. He was waiting for me to make the first move.

Realizing I had no other choice, I carefully unlocked the car doors. I kept my hands raised as I stepped out.

"Frank," I began. "Don't shoot."

34 CATHERINE

"Samuel!" I screamed into the phone. "*Samuel!*" The only sound answering my cries was the dull silence meaning the connection had been lost. I lowered the phone slowly, mind racing. What was happening? I knew that he was driving, someone had a gun, there was a man named Frank . . .

Hands nearly numb, I shakily dialed three numbers.

A gruff male voice snapped my reeling brain back into focus. "911, what is your emergency?"

"I think my boyfriend is in trouble." The words quavered as they passed my lips.

"Why do you think that, ma'am?" His tone asked me silently to remain calm. I tried my best to comply.

"I was talking to him on the phone and . . ." The words seemed almost surreal. "He said he saw someone with a gun."

"Where is your boyfriend now?"

"I don't know exactly. He said he was driving and there was some background noise, so I think he's somewhere in the city."

"What kind of car does he drive?"

"It's black. A . . . Chevy Camaro, I think he told me."

There was silence and I was terrified he had hung up. "Is it an older model?" he finally asked.

"Yes, actually. Why?"

Another pause. "What is your name, ma'am?"

"Catherine Linnel."

"Catherine, I need you to stay on the line with me. We're dispatching someone now to look for your boyfriend. In the meantime, I'm going to ask you a few more questions about that car."

35 SAMUEL

Although he didn't make it obvious, the anger Frank exuded was palpable from where I was standing. His hands were currently empty, but there were plenty of places on his person to conceal the weapon. I saw him note the people across the street with his eyes. Witnesses.

"Samuel . . ." he remarked, giving a small smile. "We don't want to do this out here, right? The entire city doesn't need to hear our private conversation." Frank gestured to my car. "How about we talk inside? To be sure we're not overheard."

Alarms went off in my head at the thought, but Frank's tone left no other option. I would have to trust he wouldn't do anything brash with those people watching. My actions seemed to happen in slow motion. I took a step back, then opened the driver's side. My heart pounded in my chest as he moved to enter the passenger's. The door seemed extraordinarily loud when he slammed it shut.

We were alone.

"So, Samuel." Frank cracked the knuckles in one hand, then the other. "Might I ask what the hell you're doing?"

I swallowed. "I'm doing what I said in the note. I told you I can't do this. Just let me go and you'll never see me again. I swear on my life I won't tell anyone anything."

Frank shook his head, reaching for something in his coat. I tensed and prepared for the worse. But he only pulled out a stack of bills. "See, your life isn't worth enough to me." He waved the bills in front of my face, mocking me. "And this $500 definitely isn't worth it. Do you think I accept bribes, kid?"

"It was for the bet," I said, feeling like every word I spoke dug a deeper hole for myself. "You won."

"There you go, talking about that damn bet again. You know, you seem awfully fixated on it, don't you agree? Here you are, jumping ship, and you're still thinking about that girl." Frank leaned toward me and I shifted away. I was sure he could hear my heart slamming against my ribcage. "I warned you, Samuel. About that girl and about you trying to get out." Looking forlornly toward me, he continued, "You had so much potential. It's a shame you forced my hand in this way."

I realized what was coming a split second before it actually happened. I threw my weight against the door, pulling desperately at the handle. It didn't budge. He had locked it from the opposite side.

No, it couldn't be like this. It couldn't end like this.

Frank was pulling something out again. "Goodbye, my Scavenger," he said. It took him seconds to aim the gun at my chest. The barrel gaped at me, staring at its desolate target. My brain vaguely made the connection that he had a silencer on the weapon. No one would be able to hear it from the outside.

I kept my eyes locked on Frank's when he pulled the trigger.

There was a muffled bang and a burst of agony. Then it all went dark.

36 NATHAN

"What do you mean, they don't know where it is?" I whipped around the corner, wheels screaming as I stepped on the gas. "Someone in this damn 'city that never sleeps' has got to have seen that car!"

The scratchy voice on the radio replied, *"We'll keep you updated, Tawallis."*

"Bunch of dumbasses," I spat, eyes skimming the view outside the windshield.

"Watch your language, please," commented Therese from the passenger seat. "And watch your turns, too. You cut that last one awfully close."

"Shut up, Therese."

She crossed her arms, put-off by my tone of voice. "Remember our agreement? Head clear, right?"

"Shut *up*, Therese."

Our bantering was interrupted by the radio. *"Black Chevy Camaro spotted, parked at East 111 and 1st."*

Reading a street sign, I swiftly turned the vehicle toward the destination. "Heading there now."

"Two men are confirmed to be inside. Caution is advised."

"10-4." I turned down the volume of the device with one hand while simultaneously flipping on a turn signal. "Therese, this is it. We've finally got this son of a bitch."

"I know, Nathan. Just remember—"

"Head clear, yes, I know." But even as I said it, my mind was racing. This was what we had been waiting for. After months of working to catch this guy, we'd finally gotten our break.

37 FRANK

I saw red. A droplet slid down the window to meet the small dots sprayed across the dashboard. I wiped specks off my glasses, placing them back on my face with slightly shaking hands. The kid wasn't moving, his skin paling to white as his shirt grew red. He should've known what he was getting himself into. I had no sympathy for the bastard. After all I had done for him, this was how he repaid me.

Knowing what I had to do, I stepped out of the car and slipped the gun back into my inner-coat pocket. I sprinted to the truck, threw open the door and stepped inside. I slammed the gas and left the scene to fade behind me.

My fingers left smears of his blood on the steering wheel.

Had I glanced into the rearview mirror for half a second, I would've seen the cop cars screeching to a halt beside the Camaro. A man and woman leapt out with their guns drawn, scanning the scene. I would've seen them immediately spot the blood painting the inside of the car and run toward the kid. The woman picked up her radio mid-stride. "Dispatch, we've got a 10-10 S."

I would've seen Samuel barely have enough strength to point in my direction before passing out.

38 NATHAN

"Where's Samuel?" the girl repeated. "Please, just tell me if he's okay. That's all I want to know."

I sat down in a chair facing her. "He's fine, Catherine. I told you he's in the hospital, getting the care he needs. Now, I'm going to repeat my question: what did Samuel tell you about himself when the two of you were dating?"

The station's harsh lights caused her to squint, exaggerating the mixture of fear and confusion lining her face. An act. God only knew the amount of information she was keeping from us. "He kept me mostly in the dark," she admitted, picking at a pull in her sweater. Nervous habit. "I could guess that there was something wrong, but I tried not to press too much."

Therese nodded with what I assumed was feigned understanding, simultaneously taking notes on her ever-present clipboard. She was tasked to take special note of any body language, repetitive movements or perspiration that could indicate false statements. Even though this girl wasn't directly involved in the shooting itself, there was no saying she wasn't otherwise tied to the case. There was no way I would take that chance. "Did he ever mention anything about the networks, or drugs in general?"

"Well . . ." Catherine shifted in her seat. Uncomfortable. "There was this one time that he — gave me . . ."

"Gave you a joint of marijuana," my partner interrupted. "He told us about what happened after prom." We hadn't told Catherine what else Samuel had told us: the joint had been what he called the Usher, a particularly addictive laced strain of marijuana. Although I did take the information into consideration, I didn't automatically take it for fact. He had lied before, and there was no stopping him from fabricating the whole thing in order to protect the girl from charges. Even so, Therese and I had made the decision to keep the information from Catherine in order to gauge her responses. If she had been in on it the whole time, as I suspected, she was already fully aware of what had occurred. I just had to wait for her to let something slip.

"That's right," Catherine agreed, then quickly continued, "but I didn't use it. And I don't understand why that's important. Loads of people have addictions. That doesn't explain why Frank shot him."

"Did he ever take you to his house?"

"Tell me what this has to do with Frank."

"Catherine." I was beginning to lose my patience. She was skirting around my questions, attempting to shift my focus. "I need you to cooperate with me and answer truthfully. Where did he take you when the two of you were alone?"

"I won't answer anything else until you tell me what really happened to Samuel. I want to talk to him."

It was the oldest trick in the book. If they met, they would be able to convey information without us knowing. Even if we listened in on their conversation, they might use a code or find another way to secretly communicate. I couldn't let that happen.

The table shook when I slammed my hand down in frustration. She jumped slightly at the noise, another sign that she was on edge. "I lay down the rules. You are going to tell me—"

"Nathan," Therese warned.

"*Where did Samuel take you?*" The girl stared at me, shocked into silence. "Sarah, *answer me!*" I stopped. "I — I mean Catherine." Catherine was her name, not . . . "I need you to answer my questions."

Therese shoved her chair out. It squeaked sharply against

the granite and the girl flinched at the sound. "I'm going to need a word in the hall, Nathan." She strode to the door without waiting to see if I would follow. I silently cursed myself and followed, knowing what was coming.

"What the *hell* was that?" Therese snapped once the door was shut. "Don't think I'm just going to let that slide."

"It was stupid. I made a mistake." I had completely lost myself for a moment. Forcing this girl to divulge information wouldn't save Sarah. It was late, far too late, for that.

"No, you didn't. You completely lost it. Sarah is gone, Nathan." At the sound of my sister's name, I met Therese's eyes. She must have read my anguish for her next words were lighter, less accusatory. "You need to face that and stop letting it consume this case."

I stabbed a finger toward the door. "I don't believe this girl. Look at her body language, her vocal intonations — she's protecting those sons of bitches." Thoughts that had long since been locked away in my mind were floating to the surface. "If she was involved in this network, there's a chance she could've been involved in others. Even the one that took Sarah."

"You think this girl is responsible for *your sister's death?* Nathan, get a grip on yourself." Clenching my hands to settle their tremors, I felt the haze of fury and pain slowly lift from my mind. "I think this girl was targeted and got sucked into this whole mess. She's a victim, not the criminal. Of course she's nervous and scared. She was just informed that her boyfriend was shot. She has no idea why. She's agitated and sleep-deprived." Mulling over the mental notes I took during the interview, I realized they fit with what Therese was saying. I had been so blinded by the prospect of Catherine being involved in the network, and possibly Sarah's death, that I never even entertained the thought that she might be telling the truth.

Therese, seeing the shift in my expression, continued, "All she wants are answers. Maybe we should give her some before we ask anything else of her. Make the final judge on her honesty once we're all on the same page."

This girl deserved a chance. If Sarah had been given a chance, she might've been able to get out before it got as far as it did. Like usual, Therese was the voice of reason. "Okay. We can try that."

My partner caught my arm when I began to walk away. "Keep your head clear, Nathan. I don't want to see that happening again."

"It won't," I assured her. It had been almost four decades since Sarah's overdose and death. Some wounds never healed completely, I knew that. Therese would begrudgingly accept my momentary lapse in focus, but I knew she wouldn't be so understanding at the next occurrence. She might have me resigned, temporarily or otherwise. Therese and I had a long history, but I knew she wouldn't let it interfere with her work.

Catherine still hadn't moved when we reentered the room. Her gaze flicked rapidly from Therese to me. My partner sat down in the seat beside her. "We've decided to give you some of the answers you're looking for." Catherine's face lit up, but dropped soon after when Therese continued, "This is going to come as a shock, so I'm going to need you to stay calm. Can you do that?" Catherine nodded uncertainly, relieved that the questions were over for the moment. "I'm assuming you're aware of the laced marijuana investigation currently underway at your school."

"Yeah, but I don't know too much about it" the girl responded slowly. "I heard they were interviewing people about it. I wasn't called down to talk, though." Terrified realization dawned on her face. "Are you trying to say Samuel was working with those people? Just because he offered me pot? He's not involved in anything like that."

"Catherine." My partner placed a hand on the girl's clasped ones. "Samuel was part of the drug network."

"No," Catherine choked, pulling her hands violently out of Therese's. "You're lying." Even as she said it, her paling features told otherwise.

"We're not," I replied evenly. There wasn't a light way to

put my next words. "He confessed to it a few minutes ago. He made a bet with his dealer to get you hooked. That's why he tried to give you the joint."

"No, Samuel loves me. He would never do something like that." Denial. That was a true enough emotional response. I heard the bravado beginning to leak from her words as the truth set in. Suddenly, I felt a swell of pity for this young girl. None of this was her fault. She was dragged into it, just like I was with Sarah.

Therese's expression was pained. "We're telling the truth, Catherine. I'm sorry."

I expected the girl to burst into tears. That would've been understandable considering the circumstances. Instead, she slowly processed the news that had been thrust upon her. Pieces were coming together in her mind. The only emotion she showed was the single tear that slid slowly down her cheek.

Catherine turned her head toward us. She seemed steeled for the worst. "What's going to happen to him?"

Impressed by her emotional control, I answered, "News will spread that he's confessed. Others involved will label him as a snitch, putting him in danger of being killed for spilling secrets. He's being placed in the Witness Protection Program for his own safety. We'll also need him for Frank's trial."

Catherine licked her lips. "I want to talk to him."

Therese and I shared a look. "I'm sorry, I can't do—"

"I want to talk to him." Her voice broke when she whispered, "Please."

My mind worked, seeing how we could use this request to our advantage. "How about this: you answer just a few more questions. Then I'll let you see Samuel. Deal?"

Narrowing her eyes at me, Catherine stated, "I want a private conversation with him." Something had shifted inside her. This was not the girl we had been talking to moments before. The frightened demeanor had completely vanished, replaced with a tight grip on reality.

"I just need some information I can use to get these assholes. Then I'll give you five minutes with your boyfriend."

Catherine moved to sit. Swiftly wiping away the remains of the tear, she nodded tersely. "It's a deal."

39 SAMUEL

When the detective walked into the room, I had been half-reading a magazine left on my bedside table. Instead of comprehending the material, I skimmed the words with my eyes and flipped the pages every couple minutes. The motions were meaningless, empty movements to fill the yawning minutes stretching into hours.

"Hi," I said, shifting with the arm not stuck with the hypodermic needle to give a small wave. I remembered her name as Therese. She seemed nice enough. The other, Nathan, had an edge to him that I wasn't fond of. Guess I'd be getting to know cops a lot more now.

Therese gave me a small smile. "Hello, Samuel." Crossing the room, she sat down gently at the foot of my bed, careful not to disturb me. "How are you doing?"

I shrugged. "Alright, I guess." Glancing down at the

bandages covering my left shoulder, I added, "Meds are working, so I don't feel much pain."

"That's good." After each of my responses she stared at me carefully for a few seconds before moving on. I couldn't help wondering if this was an unofficial interview. Contrary to that thought, she seemed sincere when she said, "I wanted to tell you how thankful I am for your willingness to give up the information."

"Thanks."

"Frank was detained a couple hours later on I-95. He's in custody."

I nodded. There was nothing to say.

Therese gave me a knowing look. "I'm sure you know what all this means for you."

Of course I did. Rather than feeling an emotion, any emotion, toward the coming events, I felt only a blank acceptance. This was what I deserved. "Yeah. Pretty much."

"Your next step is the Witness Protection Program. They'll be relocating you as soon as possible. Only when you're safe will you begin your probation. You'll be asked to be in court on account of Frank."

I forced myself to smile despite my churning insides. "I thought as much."

The detective gave me a closed-lip smile before standing. "The real reason I'm here is to inform you that you have a couple visitors. Are you feeling up to it?"

I pushed myself up in the hospital cot with one arm. Any change in scenery would've been a God-sent. "Absolutely."

"Well, the first one that arrived to see you was Catherine Linnel. The second—"

"Have her come in," I cut in.

Therese raised a brow. "I really think you should—"

"No. I want to see her first."

The detective paused before relenting. "Okay. I'll get her." She exited the room before shutting the door carefully behind her. In the minutes that passed between her return, I attempted to think of something to say to the girl whom I owed so much. No words came.

Therese returned with her walking slowly in tow. "I'll give you two some time alone," the detective said. "I'm right outside the door if you need me." She exited the room once more.

Time passed and the room stood still. It was like the lack of sound itself was a noise, filling the space between us with heavy, tangible air.

When I couldn't bear it any longer, I broke the silence. "Hi, Catherine."

"Samuel." Her expression betrayed nothing. She reminded me of stone, face cold and unforgiving. There seemed to be something different about her, something I couldn't place. She kept a distance of a few feet remained between us when she walked to the side of my cot, hands at her sides.

Leaning my head back against the board in resignation, I asked quietly, "What did they tell you?"

She blinked. "Everything."

A mix of emotions washed over me. Part of me was relieved I didn't have to see the broken look on her face when she learned the truth about what I had done. Another part of me was ashamed for feeling that way. I should've been the one to do it, to tell her. But I couldn't bring myself to do it when I had the chance. It was too late now. It was too late for a lot of things. I stared up at her, searching for some glimmer of forgiveness. But the gaze that met mine held an unwavering sharpness.

"They told me what's going to happen to you."

"I'm going to start over, Catherine," I explained hurriedly. "I'm getting away from all this, moving someplace safe—"

"So I guess this will be the last time we see each other," Catherine said. Her eyes were filled with tears. My expression must have betrayed my pain, for she said, "Please try to understand. I can't trust you anymore. I've accepted everything that happened. But you lied to me. You gambled on my life. You tried to get me addicted." She shook her head sadly. "How can I forgive that?"

I breathed deeply, chest tight. "I understand." The words sent a stab of pain to my chest. This had to be done. With nothing to lose, I decided to throw out one last line. "You know, for what it's worth, I really did love you. Even with . . . everything that was happening."

Catherine smiled sadly. "Yeah. Me too."

"You were a great dancer at prom."

"Thank you. So were you."

I took a leap of faith. "Do you want to know a secret?"

Catherine stared at me. "You have got to be joking."

"No! Not like — this is funny."

". . . Okay."

"Remember that song from *Napoleon Dynamite*?"

"Yes, we danced to it."

"I had actually practiced dancing to that same song before prom with Nickie."

"Really?" Catherine's laughter filled the room. I realized it was the last time I would hear it. "I didn't know that."

"I was going to tell you at prom, but I was too embarrassed."

Our mirth quickly dissipated. My heart sank when Catherine moved until she was standing beside me. Meeting her eyes, I said, "I'm sorry it had to be this way."

"So am I," she whispered. The machines keeping me

alive throbbed in rhythm with my heart. I hoped she was doing what I was, thinking about the good memories. I hoped she didn't let them get concealed behind the rest of the mess. "Goodbye, Samuel." Leaning down, she pressed her lips to my forehead.

And then she was gone.

40 THE BOY, AGE 17

After the girl left, the hospital room seemed emptier than it had been. The boy had never felt so alone. Sitting in the quiet, he listened to the beeping of his heart monitor. The medicine he was taking could do nothing to dull this pain.

A light was coming from the hallway. The boy looked up, seeing two familiar people enter the room. He froze in recognition. They walked to stand close to him.

"Hello, Samuel," the man said. He took the boy's hand. This time, the boy didn't pull away.

"Hi, Dad," he said softly. The boy didn't know what to think.

The woman went down on both knees so her eyes were aligned with her son's. "We started looking for you when the social worker called us, asking where you were. It was only when we didn't have the answer that everything came into focus."

"This is our fault. We should've taken better care of you. We should've cared, we should've looked for you when you didn't come home." The boy smelled no alcohol on the man's breath. "They told us what's going to happen to you. That you will be starting over in a new home."

"If it's okay," the woman said, eyes brimming with tears, "we want to start over with you. Would you like that?"

The boy looked at his parents. He remembered the alcohol, the pain, the suffering he had endured. Now, he saw their tear-stricken faces. The vulnerability in their eyes. He wanted a real family, he decided. No more running away.

Decision made, the boy nodded.

Softly sobbing, the mother drew her son close. "Oh, Samuel, I'm sorry. I'm so sorry . . ." The father wrapped his arms around them and shed a tear of his own.

The boy shut his eyes and smiled, feeling the warmth embracing him. Suddenly, the room wasn't so empty anymore.

ACKNOWLEDGEMENTS

I have no idea where to begin. So many people have played a part in helping me get to where I am today. I'm so grateful for everything every one of you have done.

The first people I need to thank are my wonderful parents. From Squigmire to Scavenger, they have been by my side no matter what. The parental relationships in this book were based in no way on my own home experiences. If they were, they would speak of nothing but love and compassion. My mom and dad have been by my side through thick and thin and I would not be writing this if not for their unwavering support.

How can I mention my family without talking about my brothers? Although we may fray each others' nerves on occasion, they have been a major part of my writing process and a constant source of inspiration for my work. Never stop being crazy!

Acknowledgement is also due to the rest of my family. Grandma, Grandpa, Nani, and Pop-Pop: thank you for everything. I know I can depend on you for anything, knowing you've always got my back. I love you guys!

Friends that have been hearing me talk about this book non-stop for months: I am so sorry for bugging you (not really), but I hope the product was worth the obsession. Special thanks to Emma, Emily, Sneha, Sarah, Kali, Hannah, Molly, Meghan, and Kristen. You're the best!

To my lovely beta readers: I love you to the moon and back! Your comments and feedback were brilliant. I cannot express what a crucial part you've played in making this book as good as it is. I am forever in your debt for the time and energy you put into making this book the best it could be.

Many years ago, a little girl handed a pile of papers to her teacher and said, "Will you read my book?" Instead of turning the child and her barely readable manuscript away, they were welcomed with open arms. This is a nod to my elementary and middle school teachers who read and reviewed my work at my request. You were, in all honesty, my first beta readers. Thank you for the support and inspiration you gave me at such a young age.

For all of the people that have inspired me in ways big and small, you're a part of this book as well. Some of your influences are more obvious than others. Some of you may not even realize that I'm writing about you. Either way, you are a part of *The Scavenger.*

I thank God for helping me utilize my gift in this creation and St. Francis de Sales for the prominent role he's played in my life. Veritas!

Finally, I thank you. If you're reading this book, you've inspired me to bring Catherine, Samuel, Frank, Nathan, and all the others onto paper. Storyteller, in my opinion, is one of the greatest titles one can hold. But the stories cannot be told if there is no one to listen.

ABOUT THE AUTHOR

J. L. Willow voraciously read everything she could get her hands on as a child and continues to this day. She was inspired by the way words on a page could capture the imagination, beginning her journey as a writer at just six years old. When she's not holding a pencil, she can be found belting her favorite musicals or studying to become a mechanical engineer. Days off are spent relaxing with her family in New Jersey.

CONNECT WITH J. L. WILLOW

www.jlwillow.com
www.facebook.com/jlwillowbooks
Instagram, Twitter @jlwillowbooks

Made in the USA
Lexington, KY
13 April 2018